P9-CFB-647

"Why were they trying to kill you?"

Troy needed to move this along. The men he knocked out wouldn't be down for long. And more could come.

"I'm not sure what's going on yet. We have to get out of here so I can figure it out. Thank you for your help." Julia and the boy took a step backward.

Troy put his hands up again, trying to put her at ease. "Wait. You can't keep running aimlessly through the woods. Do you know where you're going? You don't even know how many others are out there."

Fear flashed in her eyes. "We have to go." There was a little desperation in her tone. He couldn't risk letting them go off on their own. Especially since the woman didn't even seem sure of what she and the boy might be facing. Troy had to convince her to let him help them.

Branches cracked in the direction of the school. He didn't have to see to be sure. At least two more men were coming.

Addie Ellis lives in the Northeast with her husband, son and energetic little dog. She enjoys hiking and going to the beach with her family. Having been a teacher, she has a soft spot for children. And animals, too. For Addie, writing has become a way to find adventure while exploring new places.

Books by Addie Ellis

Love Inspired Suspense

Hunted in the Mountains

Visit the Author Profile page at LoveInspired.com.

HUNTED IN THE MOUNTAINS

ADDIE ELLIS

LOVE INSPIRED SUSPENSE
INSPIRATIONAL ROMANCE

If you purchased this book without a cover you should be aware that this book is stolen property. It was reported as "unsold and destroyed" to the publisher, and neither the author nor the publisher has received any payment for this "stripped book."

LOVE INSPIRED® SUSPENSE
INSPIRATIONAL ROMANCE

ISBN-13: 978-1-335-59929-2

Hunted in the Mountains

Copyright © 2023 by Addie Ellis

Recycling programs for this product may not exist in your area.

All rights reserved. No part of this book may be used or reproduced in any manner whatsoever without written permission except in the case of brief quotations embodied in critical articles and reviews.

This is a work of fiction. Names, characters, places and incidents are either the product of the author's imagination or are used fictitiously. Any resemblance to actual persons, living or dead, businesses, companies, events or locales is entirely coincidental.

For questions and comments about the quality of this book, please contact us at CustomerService@Harlequin.com.

Love Inspired
22 Adelaide St. West, 41st Floor
Toronto, Ontario M5H 4E3, Canada
www.LoveInspired.com

Printed in U.S.A.

He shall cover thee with his feathers,
and under his wings shalt thou trust: his truth shall be
thy shield and buckler.
—*Psalm* 91:4

To my husband and son, thank you for your boundless support and belief in me. Deneen, Michael and Jess, you are the best cheerleaders anyone could ask for. I want to thank my parents for encouraging me to always keep trying. A special thanks to Tina and Besarta, and the Love Inspired team, for making this book possible.

ONE

There was always something about the darkness of the night that left Julia Fay feeling adrift. The light of the rising sun usually lifted some of the murkiness, but tonight it felt as though the day wouldn't come. The fullness of the moon glowing over her yard, casting shadows that took on an ominous presence of their own, sent her mind to a lonely place she was desperate to forget. She needed the sun to creep over the horizon before she had any chance of going back to sleep.

Standing in front of the window over the kitchen sink, holding a glass of water, Julia saw movement toward the far corner of the yard. The bushes were tall and dense along the perimeter. It was one of the reasons she'd rented the little ranch eight months ago. The rest of the space was wide open, with no obstructions other than the old metal table and chairs on the small concrete patio. Julia put the glass down and leaned forward to get a better look. Surely, it was just a raccoon or some other nocturnal animal. A creature much like herself, unable to rest until the first hints of morning light began to lift away the night.

Her breath caught in her throat when a dark figure emerged from the bushes and ran toward her house. Her heart thundered, adrenaline flooding her veins. Why would someone sneak into her yard at this hour?

As the figure got closer, she could see the clumsy way he ran. His head kept turning back to the bushes as he stumbled forward. When he reached the patio, Julia could see he was a young boy, likely no more than ten. Her eyes darted to the back corner of the yard to see what—or who—he might have been looking for, but nothing else moved.

The boy stopped at her back door and seemed to be contemplating what he would do next. The glow of the moon gave a clear view of the panic etched in his face. He raised his fist to knock, changed his mind and then dropped his hand back to his side.

Without thinking, Julia walked into the laundry room and pulled open the back door. The boy's entire body jolted, nearly making Julia jump herself. Then she saw the scratches he'd likely acquired pushing his way through the thick bushes at the back of her yard. What would make a young boy do that to himself? And why was he wandering around alone in the middle of the night? The fresh bruise that wrapped around his upper arm made her belly clench with worry. What had happened to him? Who had hurt this innocent child?

"Are you all right? Do you need help?" Julia spoke in a gentle tone, not wanting to scare him. He was already shaky and looked ready to run.

The boy stood staring for a moment and then he turned his head to glance toward the back of the yard. His eyes were filled with fright. A feeling she had known well, but she worried his situation was more dire than hers had ever been. As a child, her home life had often felt uncertain, and sometimes cruel, but this seemed like something far worse. Sensing the need to get him out of the open, she put a hand on his shoulder and guided him inside, hoping he might tell her how he'd come to be there at this hour. He followed without protest. When she reached for the light switch in the kitchen, he grabbed her arm and spoke in a loud whisper. *"No!"*

Julia lowered her hand and stared down at him. "What happened to you tonight?"

His eyes dropped to the floor. He didn't trust her. Why would he? She was a stranger and he was clearly running from something that had scared him enough to push his body through those prickly branches.

She sat in one of the three chairs at the small kitchen table so she could be at eye level with him. "You're safe here. I won't hurt you. Please tell me what happened to you. I want to help."

The boy's stare met hers, but he didn't say a word. His expression was pained and his eyes communicated so much while revealing very little. There was something raw in the way his body shifted in place. So much anxiety and what seemed to be anger. But the longer he looked into Julia's eyes, the more she understood how much he needed her help. The mix of hope and doubt burning through his gaze left her little choice. She would protect him from whatever he was running from.

Beneath everything was something innocent that made it impossible to turn him away, as she had with everyone else for so long.

"Will you at least tell me your name?" Julia put a hand on his arm, trying to settle his nerves. The boy flinched a little, but didn't pull away.

He glanced around the small kitchen then looked into her eyes, maybe hoping to find some reassurance to quell his uncertainty. Finally, he spoke just above a murmur. "Jake. My name is Jake."

The sound of a dog barking in the distance echoed through the quiet of the night. Jake's breathing sped up. He ran over to the same window she had been watching him through. His head turned back and forth, taking in every inch of the yard.

She walked up behind him. "Is someone looking for you?"

He turned. "You can't let them in." His voice was low and anguished.

"Who? Is it your parents?" She glanced out the window and then back at him.

His eyes filled with unshed tears as he shook his head slowly from side to side. Before she could ask another question, movement came from the same corner Jake had entered through. This time, the dark figure was much bigger. As her eyes widened, Jake whipped around to see. He backed away from the window, slamming into her. Then he grabbed her wrist and pulled her down to the floor. Moments later, the back door creaked open very slowly. She had forgotten to lock it. How could that be? She never forgot to lock the doors or windows. It had become so routine, she did it without thought. Living alone had made her cautious. She pushed Jake behind her as she quietly reached for an empty glass seltzer bottle sitting next to the sink.

Julia's mind whirled with panic. She'd thought she would be safe here. That she would never have to worry about something like this in the quiet little town of Bluerock. It was the boy. Danger had followed him to her door and there was no way she would allow whatever was coming to harm him. Julia couldn't turn her back on an innocent child. She knew how awful that could be.

The familiar creaking of the subfloor under the linoleum in the laundry room sent her pulse humming in her ears. Julia closed her eyes for a moment, sending up a quick prayer that God would keep them safe, then moved closer to the doorway, waving her free hand behind her to signal Jake to stay back. She took a quick glance over her shoulder and saw he was crouching in the corner where the wood cabinets came together. She lifted the bottle over her head to one side, like a baseball bat. When a tall, burly figure moved through the doorway, she swung high. The thud of the thick glass bottle connecting with his head was followed by the large man dropping to his knees, a handgun falling from his grasp. She hadn't knocked him out, but he was temporarily disoriented.

Jake jumped to his feet and Julia ran over and grabbed his hand. She led him the short distance to the front door, stopping only to slip her feet into her sneakers, and then pulled him outside. Realizing she had forgotten to grab her car keys, she was about to go back inside when she heard the man moving through the house. She should have taken his gun, or at least moved it to where he wouldn't find it. There was nothing to do now but run. She knew the neighborhood well, and could most likely find her way through the yards if she had to. But which would be safer? The roads or the yards? And where would they go from there? Jake had said *You can't let them in.* Not him, but them. Who else was out there? And what would they do if she and Jake crossed paths with *them*?

The sky was beginning to release the darkness as the slightest hint of light moved in. Troy Walker didn't usually run this early, but something had nudged him from sleep before dawn and he couldn't just lie there. The neighborhood was well-kept and most people were friendly but didn't watch too closely. It was exactly what he'd needed when he'd come home from his final mission with the navy SEALs last year. Bluerock was a small town in the middle of the eastern side of Pennsylvania. It was tucked in along the Blue Mountain Rocky Ridge, with a little over 2,500 residents.

Troy's good friend, Leo Finley, who happened to be the chief of the town's small police force, had promised Troy he'd find a real home in this close-knit community. A place where he could put all of the darkness from his time overseas behind him. His friend had been true to his word. Bluerock was a quiet little town where very little happened. The people were quick to exchange polite pleasantries and no one seemed to have the kind of odious intentions he had seen so much of during his time working with the SEALs. Troy focused on staying in shape and keeping his yard neat. Trusting people's intentions didn't come easy for him.

Something about this morning felt different. Maybe because it was earlier than he was used to, but that didn't seem right. He continued up the hill, toward the small brick elementary school. Even though it was on a dead end, he included it in his route. He liked the idea of all those children coming to school each day with their hopes and ideals still intact. They still had their innocence. The world hadn't gotten ahold of them yet. Troy envied them for that.

As he jogged along the front of the school, on the road to the dense forest, the hairs on the back of his neck stood up. There was an energy in the air. The birds weren't even singing as they normally did at this hour. The stillness felt like a warning of something he wanted more than anything to avoid. It lurked in the darkness, filling Troy with dread. The familiar feeling triggered the instincts that he had relied on during his missions. Maybe his senses were off. He had been back in the States for nearly a year. Could he have lost some of his skills so soon?

He was about to ease into his turnaround, at the curved end of the street, when movement near the brick building caught his eye. A woman and a boy ran across the grass, into the woods, from the backside of the school. Troy stopped, feeling that familiar tension vibrating through every muscle fiber in his body. Why were they going into the woods at this hour? They weren't dressed for a hike. They both looked to be wearing pajamas. Everything about it felt wrong. A chill ran down his spine. It was exactly what he'd felt overseas right before he'd had to engage with a dangerous enemy.

Troy wanted to be wrong. Maybe his ability to read a situation was faltering. He had gotten used to the simplicity of Bluerock. He had embraced it more than he'd thought he would when he'd first arrived. Maybe he was projecting from his time dealing with the darkest dregs of the earth. The kinds of people that would make anyone question whether humanity had any real hope of staying within the light.

Two large men, carrying guns, appeared from behind the school and ran into the woods in the same direction the woman and boy had gone. Troy froze. His eyes had to be playing tricks on him. This kind of thing wasn't supposed to happen here. *Boring* was how his friend had described it last year, which had sounded perfect to Troy. He'd wanted to feel a sense of normalcy for a while. What he'd just seen was anything but normal.

He sprinted through the woods on an angle in the direction of where he thought he would intercept the men. His training gave him the ability to move quickly with very little sound. It had saved him more than once.

Troy saw the stouter of the two men first. He was tall, but a little round in the middle, making him slow. He was lagging pretty far behind the other man, who was so much faster that he had already moved much deeper into the woods. Troy eased up behind the slower man, wrapped his arm around his neck in a viselike grip, and squeezed. The man thrashed and dropped his gun, trying to pry Troy's arm away from his throat. The shock of being grabbed without warning made the man reactive rather than deliberate in his attempt to fight back, giving Troy an unexpected advantage. Troy added more pressure and pulled down, forcing the man's back to arch. When he finally collapsed from lack of oxygen, Troy started toward the sounds of the other man, who was yelling for the woman and boy to stop running.

This guy was broader and leaner, and moved with purpose. He wouldn't be as easy to take down. He was clearly better trained than the first guy Troy had encountered. Troy approached quietly, getting closer, when the man stopped to take aim. The woman moved the boy behind her to block him with her body. This could not happen.

Troy stepped up behind the man and slammed his foot into the back of his knee while shoving his shoulders with such force, his knees buckled as he fell forward, his hands outstretched to brace his fall. Troy went to kick the gun away but the guy rolled onto his back and took a shot. Troy moved to the side, but not fast enough. He felt the burn in his upper left arm as he hit the ground. Troy twisted and swung his leg to kick the gun out of the assailant's hand. Another shot rang out as his foot connected with hard metal. The gun flew into a bush. Troy spun to make sure that the shot hadn't hit the woman and child before refocusing on the gunman.

The man's face was red with rage as he jumped to his feet and started moving for the woman and boy. He was clearly determined to finish what he'd come there to do. Troy got up and went after him. After that, there was no thought. Troy's body acted on muscle memory. He moved quickly and efficiently, intent on taking down his enemy. His opponent put up a vigorous fight, and Troy began to consider he might be outmatched, especially now that he was wounded. But he knew losing meant more than his own demise.

After taking some painful blows, Troy managed to step back. His body was buzzing with adrenaline, giving him the drive to keep going. He stood staring at the man, daring him with his eyes. The man glanced at the woman and boy then came at him. Troy stepped to the side at the last second, sending him stumbling forward, and smashed the heel of his hand into the man's nose. The crunch of the break was followed by blood seeping over his mouth. Before the assailant could get his bearings, Troy maneuvered behind him and tightened his arm around the man's neck.

The thrashing and kicking might have created a challenge if Troy hadn't been so determined. There was no amount of pain he wouldn't endure to make sure innocent people stayed safe. As the man went limp, falling unconscious from lack of oxygen, Troy noticed the woman and boy watching, frozen with fear. He released the man, letting him fall to the ground, and tried to catch his breath. It had all happened in a matter of seconds, but the exertion had Troy a little winded. He immediately felt the familiar hollowness that had followed every time he had been forced to hurt someone else to survive. It was never something he took pleasure in doing. It drained him from the inside, leaving an emptiness he didn't know how to fill.

Troy ran his fingers over the wound on the outside of his shoulder. It didn't feel serious. More of an inconvenience, in his experience. Then he noticed the woman starting to back the boy away and he walked toward them, holding his hands up to show he didn't have a weapon. "I saw those men running after you with guns, and acted on instinct. I'm not here to hurt you. I just want to help. Are there any more of them?"

The boy peeked out from behind the woman, as if she could provide protection with her petite body. The woman wrapped a protective arm around him. She was clearly shaken, but there was something in her eyes. She was going to put up a fight. That was how they had made it this far. He knew that look. That stance. He had seen it in his enemies. The difference was that she was trying to protect her child, not hurt innocent people.

"I live nearby. I was out for my morning run. I can help you. Please tell me what is going on. We don't have much time before they wake up." He took a few steps closer. The woman's grip on the boy tightened. Her eyes darted around, no doubt searching for an escape route. He wondered if she knew her way through these woods.

"Don't come any closer." Her voice was strained but firm. Troy stopped. He was only ten feet away now. She looked around and then back at him. "I don't know how many there are… They're not dead?" Her voice came out a little soft. It almost seemed as if she was relieved to hear that the men trying to kill her and her son were alive. It took him a little off guard.

He took another two steps forward. "Just unconscious. But not for very long. What happened? Why were they trying to kill you?" He needed to move this along. The men he'd knocked out wouldn't be down for long. And more could come. Sneaking up and taking two of them by surprise was one thing, but taking on multiple assailants with training similar to his own wouldn't put the odds in Troy's favor.

"I'm not sure what's going on yet. We have to get out of here so I can figure it out. Thank you for your help. We need to be moving along now." She and the boy took a step backward.

Troy put his hands up again, trying to put her at ease. "Wait. You can't keep running aimlessly through the woods. Do you know where you're going? You don't even know how many others are out there. I'm guessing you also have no idea *where* they are."

Fear flashed in her eyes. "We have to go." There was a little desperation in her tone. He couldn't risk letting them go off on their own.

Especially since the woman didn't even seem sure of what she and the boy might be facing. Troy had to convince her to let him help them.

Branches cracked in the direction of the school. He didn't have to see to be sure. At least two more men were coming. Troy put his finger to his lips and quietly moved closer. The sky was beginning to lighten up. They would be easily spotted if they didn't get out of there. He should have fished that gun out of the bushes. No time for that now.

Troy spoke in a whisper. "I know these woods. And, as you saw, I'm very capable. If you'll let me help, I can get you out of here. Then you can decide if you want to tell me what's going on."

The woman glanced in the direction of the sound of the cracking branches and then back at him. It was obvious that neither trusting him nor trying to make it without him felt like good options to her. Having no time to think it through, she chose him and nodded in acceptance. The relief he felt was energizing. It gave him a sense of purpose he hadn't felt in over a year.

"Follow me closely. Don't make a sound." He led them around the dead end where he'd entered, deeper into the woods, toward the street where he lived. Going back out on the road in front of the school wasn't a viable option. There could be more gunmen there. Troy guided them, moving slowly to keep the noise to a minimum. He could hear men's voices coming from where they had been, but the sounds were fading as they continued their trek. It didn't seem as though anyone was following them.

Troy took this time to assess the people he was helping. He had so many questions that would have to wait. The boy was clearly shaken and the woman was focused on putting distance between them and those men. Plus, talking might draw attention to them. Sound had a way of carrying through the trees.

The boy had scratches on his face and arms, but looked otherwise unharmed. There was a bruise that wrapped around his right upper arm, likely from being grabbed and held too tight. Troy couldn't help but wonder if one of those men had been responsible. Exhaustion was taking over his body, making his movements sluggish. He had wavy, dark brown hair and chocolate-brown eyes.

He looked nothing like the woman. The kid either resembled his father or they weren't mother and son, as Troy had first assumed. The boy was square-jawed, with broad shoulders, and would likely be tall when he got older.

Everything about the woman was small and delicate, with the exception of the determination in her eyes. She hadn't once faltered in their trek through the woods. She swept her thick blonde hair into a ponytail without losing stride. Big, mossy-green eyes kept vigilance over the boy at all times. She had slightly full lips and high cheekbones. Her nose was small and straight, with a rounded tip. The woman was beautiful. Troy hadn't noticed her appearance before. There was something familiar about her. He just couldn't place it. For now, he needed to focus on getting them to safety. Then he could figure out how he might know her.

Once they reached Troy's road, he had the woman and boy wait inside the perimeter of the trees while he stepped out onto the pavement to see if anything seemed out of place. Those men could have people driving around, looking for them. It's what he would do in their position. Everything seemed quiet. Lights inside the houses were coming on as people were starting their day. He walked along the street, looking into the yards and windows to see if anything appeared out of sync. When he'd moved in, learning the habits of his neighbors had been one of his first priorities.

Troy was about to wave them out when he heard the crunching and snapping of twigs from within the trees. Something was moving fast. The woman looked back into the woods and turned to face him, horror in her eyes. She grabbed the boy, pushing him behind her. Troy shouldn't have walked so far from them. He tried telling her to run, but she didn't seem to hear him. If only he had at least asked her name. Then he might have been able to get her attention.

Troy sprinted toward them as a man grabbed the boy from behind her and pulled him out of sight. Another man appeared, reaching for the woman. There was no way to get to them in time. How had he let this happen?

TWO

Julia twisted her body, reaching for Jake, but her arm felt as though it was being torn off. The thought of anyone hurting that boy made her sick with despair. That man who had helped them in the woods was so far down the road. She could see him running to her, but he would never get to them quickly enough to save Jake. Without thought, Julia swung her free hand, smashing her fist into the chest of the man gripping her arm. He didn't even flinch. She tried to pull herself free, but his grip tightened. The pain radiated through her shoulder. Desperation coiled in the pit of her stomach, but something had to be done. She rammed her knee up between her attacker's legs. His hold loosened enough for her to pull away.

Her body felt heavy with exhaustion. She

had been running for so long. Then that trek through the woods. And now this. Her muscles ached, but she couldn't give in. Julia knew she had to keep going. Running faster than she ever had before, she went after Jake. When she saw the man pulling him away, she lunged through the air and jumped onto his back. He released Jake, trying to throw her off. She tightened her arms around the man's neck, trying to mimic what she had seen her rescuer do earlier that morning, but it didn't seem to have any effect on him.

"Run!" Julia screamed at Jake, but he wouldn't go. She saw him try to kick the man's leg as she was flung to the ground. The attacker reached out for Jake as her rescuer finally appeared and shoved the attacker so hard, he nearly toppled over. Jake came to her side and pulled her to her feet. She wanted to help the man who had repeatedly put himself in harm's way to help them. But how? She didn't have any of his skills and these men weren't easily taken down. Even her rescuer, who'd seemed to have an incredible amount of training, was challenged by them.

Julia could see fresh blood soaking the sleeve of her rescuer's white T-shirt. The deep red spread from the small hole on the outside of his shoulder. She had been so focused on Jake, she hadn't noticed the man had actually been shot in the woods. Was the bullet still lodged inside? How was he still fighting with such vigor with a wound like that?

The men grappled on the wet leaves, kicking up clumps of moist earth. They had taken one another down, each vying for the upper hand, and both had ended up on the ground. She looked around for something she could use to help. Anything that would stop this man from getting hurt on her and Jake's account again. Jake seemed to pick up on her thoughts and reached for a wide, flat rock. Julia took it and moved as close as she could get without being pulled into the fight. She watched, being very still, until the right moment presented itself. Then she let the rock fall onto the assailant's head and stepped back. His body dropped a second later.

The other man looked up at her with a stunned expression. He pushed himself to his feet and stood staring down at her. He was easily over six feet tall, with broad shoulders and a strong physique. Julia hadn't realized how imposing he was before. She had been so focused on getting away from the men pursuing Jake, she hadn't paid attention to what her rescuer looked like. He was lean and very fit. His hair was dark, almost black, but his eyes were a striking cornflower blue. His face was structured with an almost square jawline. His nose was slightly crooked, for obvious reasons, but somehow fit him perfectly. His lips were full and pink, aside from a little blood coming from a small split.

He reached his dirty hand out to her then apparently thought better of it and rubbed his palm on his shorts. "I'm Troy." A deeply smooth voice echoed in the quiet morning air. Blood was beginning to stream down his left arm from the bullet wound.

Julia reached out instinctively and pulled his shirt sleeve up. "I was worried it would be worse. It's only a graze. A deep one, but nothing serious. I'm Julia." She gestured at Jake as he came to her side. "This little guy is Jake." As if she had always known him. What an odd morning this had been. Three strangers coming together this way. She wondered what Troy must think of all of this. He must have at least a few theories about why armed men would be chasing her and a boy into the woods. They would likely all be wrong. Not that she could be sure. She still had very little information.

Troy's expression was unreadable. Absently, Julia reached out, tore a strip off the bottom of Troy's T-shirt, and tied it around his wound. She noticed something flicker in his eyes but dismissed it. "That should keep the bleeding under control for now."

Troy looked down at the strip of fabric tied around his arm and then at her. "Thanks." His eyebrows pulled together. "You can tell me everything when we get to my house. We should start moving before more come. You're clearly up to your neck in something. Stay close. Try to stay quiet." With that, he turned and started leading them back out onto the street.

The coldness of his tone took Julia a little by surprise. She'd thought a man who would risk his life so freely for strangers would be a little kinder. Warmer. It didn't matter. This stranger had come through for her in a way no one ever had. She closed her eyes for a moment, thanking God for sending this man to save them.

The rising sun was beginning to burn off

the morning dew, the warmth cutting through the chilly night air. Following Troy along the road shouldn't have felt so difficult. How much farther would they have to go? Julia had never had to push her body this way before.

Troy's house was at least a half mile down the road. It was mostly quiet, aside from a few early commuters heading off to work. He lived in a midsized ranch with a well-manicured yard. Every bush was perfectly shaped. His lawn was a deep green with straight edges. The house had Cedar Impressions siding with thick white trim and a white door. The backyard was a decent size with a thick row of bushes at the far end. They were also very well-kept. Inside was more of the same. Hardwood floors that appeared to be new. Cream walls without a single mark on them. Thick white moldings framed solid wood doors. The furniture was minimal, but fit the space well. There was nothing personal anywhere. It almost felt staged. Who was this man? What made him so sterile?

Julia followed Troy into the kitchen. Jake stayed close to her, clearly as unsure as she was about this man who had done so much for them. Troy pulled a first-aid kit from a small pantry closet and opened it on the stone countertop. It was better equipped than the average home kit. It contained things that wouldn't normally be found in someone's house. Unless that person was a doctor. It made her wonder why he felt the need to be so prepared. She watched him pull everything he would need out of the white-plastic box, then moved closer, finally feeling she was able to do something for him.

"Why don't you sit down and let me do this for you?" Julia stood firm as Troy looked at her with clear doubt in his eyes. "Please trust me, as I have trusted you." With that, he took a seat in one of the four chairs at the kitchen table. Again, nothing looked as though it had ever been used.

Julia cleaned the wound before starting the stitches. "Do you have anything in that kit to numb your arm before I get started?" She watched the small smirk form on his lips before he shook his head.

She shrugged and then got started. Troy watched her closely, but didn't move or show any signs of discomfort. It made her wonder what he must have endured before today to be able to handle so much. After tying the last stitch, Julia put ointment on a bandage and covered it. "Try to keep it dry for now. This will need to be changed twice a day."

Julia looked over and saw that Jake had gone into the living room to sit in a wide chair near the front window. He was staring outside, keeping watch. Her stomach tightened. How long had this boy been living on high alert? Did he ever get to be a regular kid? She tried to shake the thought away. For now, they had to focus on the more immediate problem of the men pursuing them. She turned back to Troy, realizing he hadn't said anything in response to her instructions.

He stared at her, seeming to extract something. "I feel as though I know you. I've seen you somewhere before. Do you work for the town doctor?"

The question stung a little. If her father had been there to hear it, he surely would have had plenty to say about it. "No. I sell baked goods to some of the local businesses. You've probably seen me dropping them off. I sell a lot to the diner in town."

Recognition lit Troy's eyes. "That's right. I've seen you there. Your pastries are outstanding. I haven't tried anything else, but I imagine they're just as good… How on earth do you know how to take care of a wound like that?"

Julia started cleaning up and putting things back into the kit. "My father is a plastic surgeon. He wanted me to follow in his footsteps. I went most of the way through medical school. He had me practicing stitches on banana peels when I was ten. You won't have much of a scar when that heals." She gestured to his arm. "It'll be faint for a few weeks, but it'll disappear, as though it never happened." She smiled a little, trying to hide some of the anguish she felt thinking about her old life.

"I have to ask, why would you give that up? You would obviously do well at it. And the income would be considerably more." Troy looked perplexed.

"It would be, but money isn't everything. My heart wasn't in it. I like to bake." She left it at that. No need to tell this man, whom she wouldn't likely see again, her sad little story. He didn't need to know how her parents had rejected her for her choices. He definitely didn't need to know how poorly they had treated her growing up. Jake had to be the focus. She still needed more information from him, but that would have to wait. He had curled up in the wide chair in the living room, and looked ready to doze off.

Troy stood. "Thank you for fixing me up. I should call the chief and get some cops over here to take statements."

Jake perked up and jumped to his feet. "No! You can't call the police. You can't trust them." He turned to Julia. "We have to go. We can't stay here."

"Why don't you want the police involved?" Troy walked toward Jake in that same reassuring way he had approached them in the woods. "Are you in some kind of trouble?"

"They're bad. We have to find the government guys. The ones my father was talking to." Jake edged his way closer to the front door, his eyes fixing on Julia, a plea for help in his stare.

She walked over to him and turned to Troy. "Let's take a moment here. We need more information before we get anyone else involved." She wasn't sure why Jake didn't trust the police, but there was no doubt in her mind that he must have a good reason.

"Why don't you tell me what you know? Then we can consider our options." Troy's tone was calm but a little stern.

She looked to Jake. When he nodded, she told Troy the little she'd been able to get out of Jake once they'd fled her house. "Some guys broke into his house last night and beat up his father before killing him. His mother tried to get Jake out of there, but she was shot in the yard." Jake was shrinking against her, his eyes filling with tears. She could feel him trembling.

Julia's voice dropped a little lower. She hated causing him any more pain. "Jake was forced to run off on his own. He doesn't know if his mother survived. I was in my kitchen, getting some water, when he showed up at my back door. We didn't get to talk much before one of those guys walked right into my house. We stopped at that old payphone in town and dialed 9-1-1 to get help to his mother. That's when the two you dealt with in the woods caught up with us. We had to drop the phone and run." Julia had to steady herself. Saying it all out loud gave it a heaviness she had been trying to avoid feeling. "You found us after we'd been going a little while. Thank you for that, by the way. I'm sure we'd be dead if you hadn't intervened. We owe you our lives."

Troy seemed to absorb what she'd said then

he turned to Jake. "Why did these men hurt your father? What were they after?"

Jake didn't answer. He shrugged his shoulders and moved closer to Julia. She could see the exhaustion mixing with fear in his eyes. She was glad Jake had stumbled into her yard. She didn't imagine her neighbors had her sleeping habits. What would have happened to him if he had run next door? Would that man have hurt him? Killed him? The thought sent a shiver through her body.

"Do you think we're safe here? Jake could use some sleep. And if you don't mind, I would like to try calling the local hospital to see what I can find out about his mother." Julia wrapped her arm around the boy's shoulders.

Troy motioned to the hallway. "Down the hall, on the right. He can sleep in either guest room. Then maybe you and I can talk?"

"You'll hold off on calling anyone?" Julia wanted to find out why Jake didn't trust the police before taking any unnecessary risks.

Troy looked at Jake then at her. "For now. We'll talk when you're done in there."

Julia nodded and led Jake down the hall. The rooms were neat and minimally decorated, like the rest of the house. It was hard not to wonder what Troy might be hiding from. His life seemed so solitary. It was clear he lived here alone and didn't have many visitors. What was it that had led him to live this way? Was it even safe to be with a man who could do what Troy was capable of? Could there be men like the ones she'd just run from searching for him? She paused in the doorway, considering how they could leave without him realizing. Should she risk trying to make it on her own? Would she and Jake survive the day?

Troy paced the kitchen, trying to make sense of all that had happened. What type of people was he dealing with? Who broke into a man's home and killed him in front of his child? And then to shoot his mother. This wasn't a run-of-the-mill break-in. These men were hunting this boy as though he was a real threat. It was even more concerning that Jake had mentioned his father talking to a government agency and that he didn't trust the local cops. Was it possible that Leo knew anything about this?

Chief Leo Finley had been Troy's friend

since they were teenagers. He knew the man well enough to be sure Leo wasn't behind any of it, if any of the local police were actually tangled up in this mess. But if another agency was involved, Leo could be working with them. If he wasn't aware of it, maybe he should be told that some of his guys could be dirty. It seemed unlikely in Bluerock, but Troy was used to seeing the darkest parts of humanity in the most unexpected places.

Julia's soft footsteps moved along his hallway. It had been a long time since he'd had company, with the exception of his little sister. Even that wasn't very often. He was still amazed by the way this tiny woman had fought for Jake. Especially now that he knew the boy was a stranger to her. It really said something about who she was. His instincts to protect them were right. He wouldn't desert them now, but he had to figure out how to help them.

"You need to tell me what's going on here." He spoke as Julia came into the kitchen.

"I really don't know anything more than I've told you. Jake doesn't trust easily. Whatever his father was involved in has him terrified. I had a hard time getting him to talk to me. I think he only told me about his parents because he was so upset." Julia sighed.

"He seems to trust you now. He's glued to your side. I really think we should talk to the chief of Bluerock police. He's an old friend and I trust him. I'm good at what I do, but not knowing how many of these guys are out there, we could use some backup." He was used to working with a team, not on his own. Though he sometimes chose to take certain things on by himself, hoping to protect the guys who had families waiting for them back home, his experience dictated that working as a group usually yielded a better result.

"I don't have the answer. But I know that Jake feels very strongly about it. You saw how upset he got. I know he's only a child, but he's smart and has more of an awareness than any kid should." Troy could see sadness in Julia's eyes as she spoke. Did she know that kind of pain? Had something happened to her as a child?

"You look tired. Maybe you should get some sleep, too. I'm used to running on a few hours. I'll keep watch. If I see anything that seems off, I'll get you up. There are clean towels in the hall closet, if you'd like to get cleaned up. My sister left some clothes in one of the guest room closets. She's a little taller than you, but I'm sure you can find something that fits." Troy noticed a tear in her pajama shorts. The matching T-shirt wasn't in the best shape either.

The sudden anger that filled his veins as he looked at this sweet woman was overwhelming. He wasn't used to meeting the people he saved. The idea of anyone hurting her was unfathomable. Men like the ones he'd fought off earlier were the reason he'd left the SEALs. He couldn't spend his life chasing the darkness of evil. But all that he'd seen made it difficult to see the good in people. He kept waiting for the other side to come out. It didn't feel that way with Julia. There was something dark there, but not in the same way. She was hurt. She wasn't the type to hurt others.

"Thank you, Troy. I know God brought you to us this morning. I will always be grateful that you didn't turn away when He did." The words pierced his heart. She turned to leave then stopped and looked at him. "Would you mind if I use a phone after I get cleaned up?" When he nodded, she left him to go back down the hall.

He stood, absorbing her words. He hadn't been able to sleep this morning. It was unusual. His body was stuck in a set routine. Maybe Julia was right. Maybe He did have a plan. If that was true, Troy had to trust his instincts, as that was what had guided him this morning.

Grabbing his cell phone from a kitchen drawer, he stepped outside. His backyard felt so empty now. He hadn't noticed it before, but with a kid in the house, memories of the way things had been in his childhood home were hard to ignore. He couldn't help but long for the warm summer days spent with his mother and sister by the pool or playing a game of cards after dinner. Things that hadn't entered his mind since the day his mother died.

He pulled up his contacts and dialed. Leo picked up on the second ring. "Long time no hear. What's shaking, buddy?" Leo sounded as upbeat as always.

"I need to talk to you about something serious. Do you have a minute? Are you alone?" Troy waited as he heard a door being closed.

"I'm in my office alone. What's up? I haven't heard you like this since you got back." Troy heard the squeak of Leo's chair as he presumably settled behind his desk.

Troy proceeded to tell his friend what had transpired that morning and the way the boy seemed adamant about keeping the police out of it. Troy didn't mention the possibility of another agency being involved. He wanted to hear what Leo would say first.

Leo didn't answer right away. Troy waited, knowing it was a lot to digest. "We've never had this kind of violence in Bluerock before. You know it has always been very quiet here. Someone made a 9-1-1 call in the early morning hours about what happened. There weren't many details. The boy's father was found dead. His mother is in critical condition. The doctors aren't overly optimistic right now. Troy, I need to talk to that boy. I need to know what he saw. Who he saw." Leo's tone was very serious now.

"He won't talk to you. He's terrified and he doesn't trust anyone but Julia. She saved his life. Something is off here. I hate to suggest any of your guys are dirty, but it's certainly worth looking into. Maybe the kid is wrong about that, but the men hunting him down are dangerous. I haven't gone up against guys like this since… Listen, I think he should stay with me for now. I need to keep him safe. You know I'll tell you whatever I find out." Troy felt drained. The whole thing seemed like a bad dream.

Leo was quiet again. Troy wondered if his friend would insist on bringing Jake in for questioning. "Let me do some quiet checking and I'll get back to you once I know something. Keep your head down and call me if anything else happens. I have a few guys I'd trust with my life. We can be there in a matter of minutes, if need be. Try and get Jake to talk to you. I've met him a few times. I know he's kind of a quiet kid, but I need more to go on. I'll be in touch."

Troy hung up the phone and stood for a moment, considering what to do next. It might be best to get Julia and Jake out of town until Leo could figure things out. Getting some real distance would make it easier to keep them safe. Troy was a little surprised Leo had gone along with his plan to keep Jake with him for now. It made him wonder what his friend might have known. It wasn't uncommon for Leo to be less than forthcoming about his investigations. He took his job very seriously.

"Who were you talking to?" Julia came out

the back door. Her hair was still damp from the shower and his sister's clothes were a little big on her.

Troy hesitated. He knew she would be angry, but they needed help. "I called my friend to try and get some insights."

"The cop friend you mentioned?" She didn't wait for him to answer. "After what Jake told you? I'm going to wake him and go back to my house to get my car. We can't stay here." She turned and went back inside without waiting for him to respond.

Had it been a mistake to call Leo? It seemed unlikely, but he might have lost Julia's trust, which didn't sit well. Would she really leave? He had to convince her to stay. If something happened to either of them because of his mistake, he wouldn't be able to live with it.

THREE

Julia sat on the edge of the bed in the second guest room and pulled on her dirty sneakers. How would she get Jake back to her house, on the other side of town, without being seen? It wasn't dark anymore. They couldn't slip through people's yards unnoticed. Her first thought was to question Troy's possible involvement, but he'd fought too hard to protect them. Maybe she had been too quick to dismiss his trust in the chief of police. Troy clearly had the kind of background that required strong instincts. She was too tired to consider all of the possibilities. She would leave with Jake and figure out what to do once she got her car.

She could go home. She had been estranged from her parents for a few years, but surely they wouldn't turn her away with a young boy in danger. Her father would know what to do. He always knew what to do. But did she really want to involve her parents?

"Please don't go." Troy stood in the doorway. She hadn't heard him come down the hall. How did a man of his stature move so quietly? "I know I screwed up. I don't do it often, but I realize now that I should have waited to call Leo. At least until I had more information."

Julia nodded. "I get it. You trust your friend. I trust Jake. He hasn't told me everything, but I think he will. I'm going to get him out of town—"

Troy interrupted. "That was my exact thought. We can take my truck. I'll gather some supplies and get us far away while Leo figures things out." He watched her, his expression still difficult to read. "I really don't think you should go on your own. If they catch up with you again, I don't think they'll hesitate to shoot this time. These guys aren't amateurs. They won't take the chance that you'll get away again." He leaned against the doorframe, crossing one foot over the other. He was so calm with all of this.

"What do you do for a living?" Julia watched

for anything to shift in his eyes. There was nothing. He was completely at ease.

"Right now, nothing. I help people out here and there, but I don't have a steady job. I was a navy SEAL until about a year ago. I'm guessing you're trying to figure out if I'm dangerous and where I learned to do the things you saw me do."

Straight to the point. Julia wasn't used to it, but she could appreciate that approach. "That explains a few things. If Jake and I put our trust in you, we need to know you won't make decisions unilaterally going forward. Can you handle that?"

Troy stepped inside the room and held out his hand. "I give you my word. I will discuss things with you unless it isn't possible."

Julia stood and walked toward him. She looked up into his eyes. He seemed sincere enough. His actions had indicated that he was an honorable man. Yet she had no illusions. In the right set of circumstances, he would do it again. But he was her best option. She reached out and his big fingers wrapped firmly around her hand. His skin felt surprisingly warm. There was a roughness to it that matched what she had seen of him so far. There was also a kindness in his eyes that he didn't seem to want to show. Why? What had he seen in his time with the military? Certainly far worse than what she had been through this morning.

Troy lingered, staring down at her, his eyebrows drawn together. Then he let go and stepped back. "Leo said Jake's mother is in critical condition. They don't know if she'll make it. I don't think we should bring Jake to the hospital until we know more." He watched her. When she nodded, he continued. "You should get some sleep. We'll leave at dusk. I'll gather supplies and pack the truck. I have a big SUV. We'll have everything we need. There should be a few pairs of shoes in the closet. You might have to double up the socks, but there should be a pair of sneakers that work for you." He left without another word, assuming she would follow his plan. Julia supposed she would. Troy was clearly better equipped to navigate this kind of situation.

She kicked off her shoes and got into bed. More than anything, she needed sleep. The stress of being so close to death and nearly failing at keeping Jake safe had drained her body, leaving her bone-tired.

* * *

Troy had spent the afternoon packing his SUV with everything they would need. Some nonperishable food, water, weapons, camping gear and a deck of cards. He even took a few lengths of twine and put them into his pocket. An old habit from his time with the SEALs. When he came in from the garage, there was a mouthwatering aroma in the air. An unexpected sense of nostalgia made him unsteady for a moment.

He found Julia cooking in his kitchen. She turned and smiled at him. She looked rested. Much better than the frazzled woman he'd met this morning. He hadn't realized how hungry he was until now.

"I hope you're hungry. Jake is washing up and should be out soon. The food is almost ready. I hope you don't mind, I raided your refrigerator." She had a kind voice. It reminded him of his mother. Everything about seeing her this way was reminiscent of his childhood.

"Use whatever you want. It smells amazing." Troy stepped closer to the stove, hoping to get a preview of what was coming. "You're finding your way around well." He couldn't help but smile at that thought. He liked having Julia in his house. The sentiment was unexpected.

"How do you feel about filet mignon with a balsamic glaze and roasted potatoes?" She lifted the lid off a small pot on the stove and stirred, then she held the spoon out to him. "Want a taste of the glaze?" He didn't hesitate.

"I can see why you might prefer to cook. That's incredible." Troy liked that he made her smile with his words. He hadn't done that with anyone in a long while.

Jake came out and sat at the table. Troy sat with him, hoping the boy would start to feel more at ease around him. "How did you sleep?" When Jake shrugged, Troy said, "Are you as hungry as I am? It smells really good. I think we have a master chef in the house."

Jake's expression finally lightened into a small smile. "I bet Julia's good at everything." He watched as she set plates of food on the table.

"I bet you're right." Troy decided to keep things light, hoping Jake would open up. They all stayed pretty quiet through dinner. They were all strangers to each other, thrown together…by God? He wondered if Julia had been right about that. He had lost his faith, but today, in spite of what he'd seen, there was no denying the possibility that he hadn't happened upon them by accident. The possibility that he had been drawn to this little town to serve a purpose centered his mind. He had been floating along with no sense of direction and he hadn't liked it.

The sun had set by the time Troy had helped Julia clean up the kitchen. He kept the lights off in the front part of the house, with the curtains drawn. The light over the stove was the only one on. Leo had given him an update on Jake's mother. She was stable, but it was still unclear whether she would survive. Jake was relieved to hear his mother was alive, but disappointed that he couldn't see her. He settled into the same wide chair he'd occupied earlier that day.

Troy noticed Julia watching the kid with concern. She would make a good mother one day. "We should get going. It's dark enough, so they won't see us inside my truck. The windows have some tinting, but not dark enough to hide us during the day. We should be good now."

Julia nodded and started for the living room when Jake came flying in and spoke in a loud whisper. "Someone is here. There's a bright light outside." He was breathing heavy, as if he had been running. The idea of this kid being put through so much was enraging.

Troy moved quickly down the hall into one of the guest bedrooms. He stood back, so he wouldn't be seen, and peered through the white sheer curtains hanging over the window. Three men were converging on his house. A pickup, with oversized tires, was parked in the middle of the street, shining a row of lights fixed on the truck's roof at his house.

He moved quickly through the house, grabbing Julia and Jake by the hands and pulling them out the back door. They followed him at a full run toward the bushes lining the back of his yard. As they moved inside, Jake tripped, making a little too much noise. One of the men he'd seen out front ran their way and stopped, his gun raised, and surveyed the area. He kept very still, waiting for another sound so he could shoot in that direction. The silencer on the weapon made it clear he was prepared to kill right here. Would he just start shooting? Jake was nearly panting. The man was going to hear.

For the first time in a long time, Troy's heart beat heavily in his chest. He was with civilians, not soldiers who'd signed up for danger. He'd never felt this helpless before. The gunman seemed to be getting into a stance when the neighbor's cat jumped out of the bushes with a screech. The man pointed his gun at the cat. Would he hurt an animal? He made a mock shooting noise with his mouth and then walked back through the yard, to Troy's house. Troy slumped with relief. That could have easily ended a very different way. Thankfully, it hadn't. Was it possible that God was looking out for them? That cat never usually ventured out of his own yard.

"Stay very quiet and move slowly. We want to keep the noise down. If that guy comes back here again, I'd bet he shoots first and looks later." Troy led them through the bushes that lined the sides of the two neighbors behind his yard. He had done it before, to make sure he had another route out of his house. But he'd never expected to use it. They had to crawl along the dirt to avoid getting scraped by the branches. The area in the middle was sparse due to the lack of sunlight. It made for a convenient escape tunnel.

When they emerged on the road, Troy realized everything, including his truck, was back inside his garage. They had nothing. No food. No transportation. No weapons. And they couldn't stay out on the street. It would only be a matter of time before those men figured out they had slipped away and started searching. But where would they go? And how would they pay for it? All he had in his pocket was the twine he'd cut into sections earlier and his cell phone.

It felt as though they had been walking for hours. How long had it really been? Julia didn't have the conditioning for this. Her legs were tired. Her feet hurt from wearing sneakers that were a size too big. The cold, damp air chilled her to the bone. Troy had led them through various yards and back into the woods. The idea of it terrified her. The woods might not ever be the same for her after all of this. At least the sky was clear with a three-quarters-full moon. It provided plenty of light, making the forest feel slightly less eerie. Jake stayed close, clearly as shaken as she was. Troy led with his usual calm. It seemed like the norm for him. Once they were far enough away from any houses, she decided to ask what his plan was.

"Where are we going? Do you intend to sleep in these woods?" The idea sent a shiver through her body.

"No. There's a farm about a half mile from here. Without the truck, it's kind of hard to get anywhere. I know we've been walking for a while, but I figured we'd be safer coming through the woods. Those guys are probably doing a grid search of the streets right now. It's what I would have my guys doing."

What he would have his guys doing? It was easy to forget that Troy was very similar to the men pursuing them in certain ways. Julia was glad to have him on her side. She thought about asking to stop and take a break, but it was only a little farther. It would be better to get out of sight. Any delay could put them at risk. Had Troy lived this way often during his time as a navy SEAL? Was he numb to the feeling of fear from danger?

"It's up ahead. We'll be exposed as we cross the field. We need to move quickly." Troy picked up the pace, forcing Jake and

Julia to keep up. The farmhouse was dark. Was that where they were going? Was it empty? The land appeared well maintained, as though someone took care of it.

They moved quietly through the field, passing the house, heading for a barn that was considerably bigger. As they reached the double doors, lights shone across the field, in the direction of the little farmhouse. Troy pulled them inside and pushed the door closed. He stood very still, prompting her and Jake to do the same. Light filled the cracks around the doors and beamed through windows above. Julia's pulse hummed in her ears. The light didn't move. Were they going to come in? These could very well be her last moments on this earth.

FOUR

Gravel crunched under the tires of the truck outside. It was rolling slowly toward the barn, the light becoming more intense. *God, please don't let it end this way. Jake is so young. Please help us.* Julia's eyes were closed, her hands clasped tightly together under her chin. She wasn't sure how much more of this she could endure. She couldn't help but contemplate what kind of emotional damage all of this would cause Jake. He was only ten. If they survived, would he have nightmares for the rest of his life? He had seen so much violence in the course of one day. And Troy kept putting himself in harm's way to protect them. She couldn't live with something happening to him because of it.

She felt Troy's hand on her shoulder. He pulled her against him, holding her body close to his. She hadn't realized she was shivering until his warmth calmed the chills shuddering over her skin and through her bones. She reached for Jake and he folded into her arms. Even with the possibility that men with guns were about to push their way in, she felt a little safer in Troy's arms. She knew he would fight for them. And that it was all in God's hands. Her worries wouldn't change the outcome. Only He could intervene.

The sound of a cell phone ringing echoed across the field. The truck windows must have been open. A man's voice could be heard, but not clear enough to catch the actual words spoken. Then the truck abruptly pulled away, casting the barn into darkness. Julia had never been so happy to be in the dark. For the first time, it was a source of relief rather than something she dreaded. She leaned into Troy as she tried to calm her erratic pulse, inhaling deeply. She held Jake tight, hoping to give him the same comfort Troy was giving her. The last twenty-four hours felt more like a week. So much had happened. It was overwhelming to even think about.

Once the truck was gone from the property, Troy looked around while Julia stood with

Jake. If only he would confide in her, maybe then she would have some idea what needed to be done to put an end to this madness. None of it felt real. It didn't seem possible that it was happening out in the open like this. Hadn't anyone noticed? Why weren't there sirens from the police coming to check on the calls from all over town? Surely, someone had to have seen or heard some of this. No one had heard the gunshots in the woods this morning? Troy's neighbors couldn't have missed the blinding light coming from that truck parked in the middle of his road. Or the three armed men surrounding his house.

"Hey, over here. I found some clean horse blankets and fresh bales of hay. We can make beds out of them." Troy was pulling the hay around, setting it up.

They walked over as Troy placed two blankets across a grouping of hay bales. Then he folded one up and put it at one end, like a pillow. "Jake, you can use this as a bed. You need to rest. We'll have a lot of walking to do tomorrow."

Jake reluctantly climbed in between the blankets. "My dad was a cop. His friends killed him when he wouldn't go along. We can't trust them, Troy. You can't call your friend again."

Julia was as stunned as Troy looked. "Jake, your dad was a policeman before he died?" She was beginning to see why he didn't trust anyone. Seeing his father gunned down in their home, when he was supposed to represent the law, had to cast doubt in the boy's mind.

Troy sat on the edge of Jake's makeshift bed. "I wish you would have told me that, buddy. The more you tell me, the better I'll know how to help you. Is there anything else you can think of?"

Troy was gentler with Jake than she would have expected from someone like him.

"No, I don't think so. I'm tired." Jake tucked himself under the blanket, turning away from them. This wasn't going to be an easy process.

Troy set up an area to sit, a small distance from Jake, and put the last horse blanket over the hay. "We can sit here. There aren't any more blankets to make beds."

"That's fine. I'm glad you made Jake comfortable. Well, as comfortable as one can be sleeping in a barn." They both sat. "Troy, did your friend mention that Jake's father was a cop?"

Troy shook his head. "No. I'm not sure what to make of it. It could mean anything. Maybe nothing at all. He knows I don't know many people here, so he may not have thought it would be relevant… But I did mention that the kid thought the cops were dirty. You'd think he would have said his father was one of them."

"Is it possible that your friend is a part of this?" Julia hated even suggesting it. She knew Troy trusted the chief.

He sat for a moment, staring out into space. "No. Not Leo. I'm sure he had his reasons. He's not the type. I've known him most of my life. It is possible that he isn't telling me everything he knows. He takes his job seriously. If he has an investigation going, he won't risk compromising it to give me answers." He thought a moment. "Do you know which agency Jake's father was talking to?"

Julia looked over at Jake. She could hear his soft snores. "No. Sorry. I'm learning it as you do now. Whatever has been going on has that boy wound tight. Maybe his father was involved. Maybe he was fearful of the man.

Maybe he eavesdropped and knew things he shouldn't have. Whatever it is, we won't know until he's ready to tell us. And if we pressure him, he'll probably clam up."

They sat quietly for a long time. Julia's thoughts were scattered. The mysteries surrounding this situation were like a puzzle with missing pieces. There was a lot of uncertainty about how it would turn out. She couldn't help but consider that she might not see her parents again. That she wouldn't have the opportunity to attempt some form of a reconciliation with them. And what about Troy? Who was he, really? She knew he had a sister. Julia was wearing her blouse and jeans. But was there anyone else in his life? Was there someone he cared for? Who might be missing him right now?

Troy's voice broke the silence. His tone was somber. "Men like them. It's why I left the SEALs. I can't believe any of this is happening here, in Bluerock, Pennsylvania. What are the odds?" He slumped back.

She reached out and put her hand over his. "Do you want to talk about it?"

Troy glanced at her then straight ahead. "I wasn't always like this. I had never known violence. I was a normal guy. My mom died suddenly when I was seventeen. We were close, the three of us. Really close. My sister and I had to go live with my aunt. She was fine, but it wasn't the same. My mom had this way about her. She could make everything better. When I turned eighteen, I signed up to the navy."

He seemed to be remembering something. Julia squeezed his hand. "It wasn't long before I got tapped to join the SEALs. I had the size and the skills. It turns out, I was built for this. It's just… I don't feel right about it sometimes. I know we need to look out for the people who can't do it for themselves, but it got really dark at times. All we did was hunt down the evil in the world. It became suffocating. Like there was no light left. No clean air to breathe."

Julia pulled him to her, wrapping her arms around this big man with a gentle heart. Something she hadn't expected. "I really believe God has a plan for you. I don't know what it is, but there's a reason you went through that dark time. A use for the things you learned. I know Jake and I would be dead without you."

She rubbed his back as he relaxed against her. "You made a choice during a time of grief. Maybe you saw some really awful things, but you also spared the world from those people continuing to hurt others. You're a good man, Troy. It may not feel that way right now, but you'll see it one day. God will put something in your path and it will be made clear why you were given these gifts."

Troy pulled back and stared at her with disbelief. "You think I have gifts? You looked terrified the first time you saw me."

"Well, you had just choked a man who was about to kill me. I wasn't sure what your intentions were." She smiled at him. "But you have showed so much selflessness." She took his hands in hers. "I have never known anyone who would have come through for me that way. Not even family. Don't ever doubt yourself. You protect people who can't protect themselves. There's honor in that. You should feel good about who you are and what you can do."

Troy pulled her close and held on. "I've never been able to talk to anyone about any of this. Not even with my sister, although she has tried. Thank you for your kind words."

She pulled back. "They aren't just words." Her eyes felt moist, thinking of the way Troy saw himself. He was a hero and he seemed to think he was something less. She felt his hand on the side of her face and she leaned into it and closed her eyes. There was so much comfort in his touch. So much more to him than she would have thought. She opened her eyes and stared up at him. He was a beautiful man. Not only on the outside, that was easy to see, but on the inside.

Troy pulled her against him. "You're shivering. The temperature is dropping. Jake should be all right between those thick blankets." He glanced over at the boy. "Let me keep you warm." He rubbed his hand up and down her arm as she rested her head against his chest. "I'm always hotter than most. Another one of my oddities." He pulled her tighter against him. "Get some rest. We have a trek ahead of us in the morning. I'll keep watch."

"You can wake me if you get tired. We can take shifts." Julia snuggled in, her body beginning to feel warm.

"I will." She knew he probably wouldn't. Hopefully, she would wake up in a few hours and get him to go to sleep. For now, she couldn't help but give in to the exhaustion consuming her. She could feel her body loosening as she began to drift into slumber.

With Julia asleep in his arms, it didn't feel like anything bad could happen. It was as if they were two people in a normal situation, getting to know each other. Except that they were hiding from killers, in a barn. Troy looked down at her. Could she be right? Could there be something useful from his years in the military that would become clear one day? She'd made him feel something besides anger for the first time in over ten years. In that moment, he actually felt okay with who he was. Not ashamed. He had always wondered what his mother would have thought of who he'd become. She'd been so much like Julia. Maybe she would have been proud.

He couldn't focus on that now. He had to make a plan. Would those men be watching his house? The ideal thing would be to go back and get his truck. It was already packed and ready to go. Assuming nothing had been done to it. Maybe Julia and Jake could stay here. If they kept out of sight, they would be safe for a little while. He could move a lot faster on his own. And if he came across those men, it would be easier if he only had to defend himself. The idea of anything happening to either of them…it would kill him. But he didn't think he'd be able to leave them alone. That was too risky.

Why wouldn't Jake open up? He had to know he could trust them now. Hadn't they proven that? He wondered if Leo had called with any updates. He had shut off his phone in the bushes behind his house, not wanting to risk the possibility of it ringing at the wrong time. Now he would have to wait. He didn't want to wake Julia or Jake.

His eyelids were getting heavy, but he couldn't go to sleep. He looked down at the tiny woman resting in his arms. Her soft blonde hair fell across her face. He tucked it behind her ear. Her creamy skin didn't have a mark on it. But she was willing to fight for that boy. She was pretty bold. Like some of the men he'd served with. His sister's clothes draped a little on her slim frame. They would probably get along well. It was a silly thought. It was unlikely that they'd ever meet. He imagined Julia would want to get as far as possible from this place once this fight was over. She may have been able to see good in him, but that didn't mean she wanted to be in his life. The whole train of thought was absurd. He would chalk it up to exhaustion.

Troy sat in the quiet, trying to formulate a plan, for hours. No one had come back. There hadn't been a flash of light or any sounds other than an owl in the distance. The first hint of sunlight was cracking through the darkness. It wouldn't hurt to close his eyes for a minute.

"Wake up!" A stern voice pulled Troy from sleep. A bright light was in his eyes. The morning sun was stitching rays through the cracks in the walls. "What are you doin' in my barn?" That deep voice again.

Troy blinked a few times, trying to focus. He could still feel Julia against him. He heard Jake stir. He squeezed his eyes closed and opened them, trying to focus. That's when he saw the double barrel of a shotgun pointed at his face.

FIVE

It was a Stoeger. Normally, Troy would have disarmed the man immediately, but Julia was still tucked against him. He couldn't risk the gun going off and hitting her. It wouldn't be like the handgun graze he had. It would blow a big hole at this range. A deadly one.

Had he gone to the wrong farm? He'd thought this was where Henry told him to stop by some time. They didn't know each other well, but Troy was certain the man was decent. He rubbed his eyes, trying to focus. Too little sleep and so much exertion had left him groggy and his eyes weren't cooperating. He felt Julia shift and startle.

"Sir, we don't mean any harm. I thought I knew…"

"Troy?" The man lowered his weapon. "I

didn't realize it was you. What are you doin' here? Are you all right?"

"I've been better. I'm sorry to show up unannounced and to stay without permission. This wasn't planned." He felt Julia sit up beside him.

"What happened? I see you brought some friends." The old man took a step back.

Troy pulled himself up, helping Julia to her feet beside him. Jake appeared at her side a moment later. "It's a long story for another time. We'll get going and leave you to your day."

"Nonsense. You'll come on inside and I'll fix some breakfast. Why don't you introduce me to your friends?" He draped the gun over his shoulder. He wore denim overalls and a flannel shirt. His hair was all white and topped with a worn baseball hat from the local high school.

"Of course. Julia, Jake, meet Henry Douglas." Troy hadn't planned on still being in this barn when Henry woke to do his morning chores. The last thing he wanted was to involve anyone else in what was happening.

"It's very nice to meet you." Julia held out her hand. Henry shook it. "I'm very grateful for the use of your barn. I hope it's not too much of an inconvenience for you."

"Nonsense. No problem at all. Come on inside. We'll get some chow. It'll be nice havin' some company for a change." Henry turned and led them toward his little white farmhouse.

Julia glanced at Troy, seeming to look for some kind of indication from him. He gave a slight nod. She accepted it and followed with Jake by her side.

Inside, the house was tidy, with pictures of Henry and his late wife in every room. There was a warmth in the simplicity of the way the rooms were decorated. Clearly, a woman's touch. Once they reached the kitchen, Henry told them to sit down at the table as he started pulling eggs and juice from the refrigerator. The space was a little tight. The round table and six chairs took up the center of the room. The cabinets were white with butcher-block countertops. The appliances were old but in good condition. Above the sink, there was a small window with white-and-yellow-gingham curtains pulled back with matching ties.

"Would you like me to do the cooking? It's the least I can do after sneaking into your barn last night." Julia stood near the stove.

Before Henry could answer, Troy interrupted. "You may want to take her up on the offer. She's quite the chef." He nearly laughed at the way Julia's cheeks blushed.

"That'd be fine with me. I haven't had a woman cookin' for me since my wife died." He took a seat at the table, across from Troy.

"What would you like?" She moved to the refrigerator.

"Surprise me. I'm not fussy." Henry leaned back in his chair.

Julia got to work. "You keep a neat home. It's lovely."

"The decoratin's all my wife. She kept it neat. I know she'd like her house to be kept the way she'd left it. She loved this place. She would have loved havin' you folks here for a visit. She always liked surprises and makin' new friends." He sighed, lost in his memories.

Troy watched Julia pull out what she needed and get things going. He and Henry talked about game night at the lodge while they waited. He was a little surprised not to be questioned about why they'd been sleeping in Henry's barn.

It didn't take long before there were plates of eggs with stacks of pancakes placed in front of them. Julia hadn't used a mix. She'd made the pancakes from scratch. The eggs were lightly seasoned and the syrup was warm. There were fresh cups of coffee with an amazing flavor he was sure she'd added, and orange juice for Jake. It was quickly becoming obvious why she'd chosen to leave the medical profession in favor of cooking and baking. She clearly loved doing it. When they'd finished, Julia stood and started clearing the table. Jake brought his dish over to the sink to help.

"You don't worry about cleanin' up. You did the cookin', and you're my guest. I'll do the cleanin' up. I still have my wife's clothes if you want to get freshened up and changed. The boy could probably wear her sweats." Henry was a kind man.

"Are you sure that's all right?" Julia put the dishes in the sink and turned to face Henry.

"It's what she'd've wanted. Now go on down the hall to the bigger bedroom. It's the closet on the left. You help yourself. Shoes, too, if you need 'em." He turned to Troy. "You and I can do some talkin' while they get cleaned up and changed."

"Thank you, Henry." Julia led Jake out

of the kitchen, glancing back at Troy before going through the doorway. He smiled at her, which seemed to give her the reassurance she needed. She was clearly out of her depth with all of this. Taking shelter and clothes from strangers probably felt odd to her. He wondered where Julia was from and who she had in her life. She hadn't mentioned needing to call anyone to check in. Didn't she have any family? Anyone who might become concerned when they didn't hear from her?

Once they were alone, Henry didn't hesitate. "Now, Troy, you tell me what you've gotten yourself into. Is that woman in some kind of trouble?"

"It's the kid, actually. I'm not sure what happened yet. I just know that some dangerous men have been trying to kill them since yesterday morning. His father is dead and his mother is in the hospital." Troy leaned back in his chair.

"I've seen the boy around town. His daddy's one of the local cops. He's dead?" Henry was old, but his eyes were still clear.

"That's what Jake said. I spoke to Leo and he confirmed it."

"Hmm." Henry looked down for a moment

then back at Troy. "You need to get them far from here. This town…" There was a banging on the front door. Henry looked uneasy as he stood and walked into the living room.

Troy moved against the wall, to keep out of sight but close enough to hear. Henry pulled the front door open. Troy wanted to look but couldn't risk it. He hoped Julia and Jake wouldn't come walking out now.

"Good morning, Officer. What brings you out this way so early?" Henry spoke in his usual relaxed way.

"Have you seen anything unusual last night or this morning? Anyone coming around who shouldn't be?" The cop sounded close, as if he was practically inside.

"No. I've been here alone all night. I'm about to start my daily chores. Just had a little breakfast. Would you like a cup of coffee? I made a fresh pot." Would Henry invite him in?

"No thanks, Mr. Douglas. I already had three cups. It's been a long night. You're sure you haven't seen anyone coming around? Even someone you know?" The cop seemed to be getting frustrated. He was clearly hoping to find them here. Maybe Jake was right about some of the local cops after all. He would have to check in with Leo to see what he'd found out.

"You sure? I know I don't make it as good as my wife did, but it'll wake you up."

"No, I'm fine. I need to check a few more places. Give me a call if anyone shows up." Troy could hear the cop take a step on the creaky wood of the porch floor. Did Leo have one of the guys he trusted trying to help? Or was this about tying up loose ends?

"Maybe if you tell me who you're lookin' for, I'll know if I need to call you. Did somethin' happen in town? Anything I should be worried about?" Henry should have let him leave. What was he hoping to accomplish?

"There's a woman and a boy I'd like to talk to. They could be in some danger. You keep your eye out and let me know if you see them."

"Of course. I'll be sure to do that. You be careful now."

"How about Troy Walker? When was the last time you saw him?" Troy's pulse spiked at the mention of his name. They knew who he was? Who were these people?

"Troy? Let's see, it's been a bit. I think the last time was game night at the lodge. That must be at least three weeks now. Is he mixed up in somethin'?" Henry had a leisurely way of talking. Troy had always thought he was a little slow, but now he realized it was Henry's way of keeping people from seeing how keen he really was.

"Nothing to worry about, Mr. Douglas. Just covering my bases. You have a good day." There was more creaking on the porch.

"None of that 'mister' business. You call me Henry." The cop didn't say anything in response. A moment later, Henry closed the door.

Troy moved quietly to the window to get a look, standing back in the shadow of the corner. He could see the officer getting into his car. He was scanning the house, likely checking for movement in the windows. Then he pulled out his phone and made a call. Troy could see the man shaking his head as he spoke. Then he drove away.

Troy turned and saw Julia standing there in fresh clothes. She looked worried. "That cop was looking for me and Jake, wasn't he?"

Troy nodded then turned to Henry. "You practically invited him in. What if he'd taken you up on your offer?"

"If I hadn't offered him coffee and tried

askin' why he was really here, he would've known somethin' was off. Everybody knows I make the worst coffee. I knew he wouldn't want any. And everyone knows I'm a busybody. If I didn't ask nothin', he woulda been wonderin' if I was hidin' somethin'. Troy, you need to get these two somewhere safe. But you won't have much luck tryin' to leave town. You know how to survive other ways. Get them hidden."

Jake came out. He was cleaned up and wearing a gray sweat suit, the arms and legs a little long on him. "They found us?"

Julia squatted down and looked up at him. "No. They were checking around, hoping someone saw us. Henry didn't tell him anything. We're fine." She rubbed his arm.

"Troy, you get cleaned up and I'll give you somethin' of mine to wear. We're about the same size. You can use my old Jeep. It'll get you where you need to go. Hurry now. You should get goin' before another one of 'em comes round." He led Troy into the bedroom and gave him a change of clothes and a first-aid kit so he could clean his wound. Henry seemed eager to get them on their way. What did he know? Certainly more than what Troy had told him.

* * *

The Jeep was in the barn where they'd slept. It had been covered by a dusty old tarp in the corner. Julia hadn't even noticed it. It didn't have a top, so they would be out in the open. Still, it had to be better than walking everywhere. Henry's wife's clothes fit her better, including the sneakers. She'd been able to find a pair that was barely worn. There were so many ways that everything could have gone differently. Not that anything about this had been easy. Still, she couldn't deny that everything they needed kept being provided. Food, shelter, clothes and now transportation. The mix of gratitude and fear prompted her to close her eyes and pray. *Thank you, Lord, for always providing. Please let this be resolved without anyone else getting hurt. Please keep us from harm while we face whatever comes.*

Jake came over and asked, "Where are we going?"

Julia opened her eyes and kept her voice low. Henry was helping Troy load the Jeep with supplies. He had packed a cooler full of food and water for them. He really was a kind man. "I'm not sure. Maybe Troy has a plan." She wished she knew more about the area. She had been so focused on her baking, she hadn't taken the time to become more familiar with the town or the people who lived there. With the exception of her customers, she had inadvertently isolated herself. Not that she had ever expected to find herself running from men intent on killing her.

Jake looked over at the men talking then back to her. "I want to see my mom. She must be worried about me."

She pulled him against her and kissed the top of his head. "I know this is really tough. If there's a way to do that, we will. I can't promise anything right now. The most important thing is keeping you safe. I know your mother would feel the same way." She could see the disappointment in the way he slumped, but she couldn't take any risks with his life. "Jake, can you tell me a little more about what happened? Or maybe why it happened?"

Jake took a step back and looked down at the floor. Then he shoved a hand into the pocket of the gray sweatpants he was wearing. Panic flashed in his eyes and his body became rigid. He ran over to the Jeep and pulled his pants out of the bag Henry had given him. He checked all of the pockets before coming back to Julia.

"I lost it. We have to find it." The anguish in his voice, the way his eyes clouded with panic, sent Julia's heart into her throat.

"What did you lose?" She kept her voice down. She still wasn't sure how much to let Henry know. There was no reason to put him at risk. He had already done so much for them.

"The zip drive. The one my dad made. We have to find it. You don't understand. We have to get it back." Jake was shifting in place, full of the same distress and anger she had seen when he'd stood in her kitchen.

"Do you know where it is?"

He shook his head, keeping the movement small. This boy was used to being subtle. To keeping things quiet. How long had this been going on? More importantly, what was this all about? He shifted behind her when Troy and Henry walked over.

"We should get going." Troy gestured at the Jeep. Henry pulled the big barn doors open as the three of them got into their seats. She noticed Troy eyeing them, clearly aware that something had happened.

As they drove outside, Henry walked over to the driver's side. "Don't try gettin' out of town on the normal roads. They have watchers all over. It'd be best to go into the woods or up the mountain. You could probably cut over somehow from there." He slapped the hood with the palm of his hand and stepped away. "Good luck to you."

Troy drove off, slowly at first, looking back at the old man a few times before speeding up. He seemed lost in thought. Julia would ask about that later. Right now, they needed to figure out where this zip drive was. It was clearly important. Jake wouldn't be so upset otherwise.

"We have a problem." Julia was reluctant, knowing Troy probably already had a plan. It would have to wait.

"I knew something was up. What happened?" Troy slowed the Jeep along a section of the long driveway littered with big dips and waves.

"Jake lost a zip drive his father made, but isn't sure where. I get the feeling it's very important. We ran a lot. It could be in your house. Or mine." Julia had no idea. Traipsing around town wasn't a good idea. How would they even begin to figure out where it could be?

"Jake, do you have any idea where you may have dropped it? We've covered a lot of ground." Troy glanced at Jake in the rear-view mirror.

Jake shook his head and spoke a little low. "No. Last time I saw it was when my mother handed it to me and I put it in my pocket. I didn't even have the chance to push it all the way in."

"So, it could be in your yard." Troy looked at him in the mirror and Jake shrugged.

They all sat quietly as Troy drove along the winding road leaving Henry's farm. Troy stared straight ahead. Julia wanted to ask more questions, but Jake was so upset about losing the zip drive, he probably wouldn't answer much.

Troy must have had the same idea. "Jake, I know you're not ready to tell us everything yet, but can you tell me what's on the drive? I need to know how important it is before we put ourselves back out in the open to find it."

"It has proof," Jake answered.

"Proof of what, buddy?" Troy was patient with him. Julia admired that about him.

They hit a rut and the Jeep bounced, sending the cooler smacking into the side of the roll bar. Something inside shifted and made a small tapping sound. It triggered a memory for Julia. "Wait. When Jake and I were leaving my house, I stopped to put my sneakers on by the front door. I heard something hit the floor. I didn't think anything of it at the time. It was something small, by the way it sounded. We could check there first."

Troy looked at her for a moment. "How likely do you think it is that that was what you heard? Going to your house is a big risk. They could be watching it."

"We could wait until it gets dark. We could park around the corner and slip in through the backyard. We could watch from the bushes for a while before we go in." Julia was shocked to even be thinking that way.

Troy's smirk was small but clear. "Things aren't always that easy. We don't know what strategy these guys are using or how many of them are out there. Maybe I should give Leo a call before we make any moves."

"No! Please, Troy, don't call the police." Jake leaned forward, practically pushing himself between them.

"Fine, I'll check the area, but if anything looks off, we're gone. It would be better if we had some backup. Some guys looking out for us while we…" Troy stopped talking as he stared into the rearview mirror. "Get down. We might have some company."

Julia hunched as she turned to Jake and pushed his head down. He curled up on the floor between the passenger seat and the back seat. She peaked out and saw a pickup coming fast. A moment later, the truck was practically on their bumper. The windows were tinted, so it was impossible to see who was inside. The truck lurched forward, nearly bumping the back of the Jeep. Troy pushed down on the gas pedal, but the Jeep didn't have much power. The pickup sped up and came alongside them, then slowed enough to drive side by side. There was no outrunning the truck. It was newer and faster. The trees were too dense to turn off the road. There was nowhere to go.

SIX

The humid morning air felt heavy in Julia's lungs, the piney scent of the trees thick in her nose. Her pulse was pinging through her ears, more of a swish than an actual beat. Some long branches formed a covering above the road, giving the feeling of being closed in. There was no way out.

It was the first time in two years that she actually missed home. The security of it. So much had happened in such a short time. It was a different kind of fear than what she'd grown up with. There was no threat of death with her parents. This was decidedly worse. She was so tired of the uncertainty. The fear of anticipating how things might get worse. It had been paralyzing for most of her life. She thought she had escaped it, but these moments of terror had been a vivid reminder of what she ran from.

Julia watched Troy move his hand slowly between his seat and the center console. When he eased out, a gun was wrapped in his fingers. He was always ready. Always had a move to make. What was that like to have a mind that worked so fast under pressure?

The dark window of the passenger door started going down. Something dark glinted in a stray flick of sunshine. Her chest felt heavy. The window dropped inside the door, revealing a black vaping pipe and two teenage boys. The engine revved again. Troy lowered the gun back down between his seat and the console. He smiled and shook his head. The boys turned forward with disappointment. A moment later, the truck launched forward, kicking up dirt as it propelled down the road ahead. Julia put her head in her hands and took a few steadying breaths. Just kids looking to race. Of all the times for that to happen.

Troy kept driving, seemingly unfazed by any of it. He turned toward the back seat. "Jake, you can get up now. They're gone."

Jake got back into his seat. "Where are we

going? We have to find the zip drive." His voice was laced with urgency.

What was on that drive? Would it put an end to all of this?

Julia looked at Troy. He nodded. "Yeah, I don't really know where to go yet. It'll give me some time to come up with something. And we obviously need to find it."

The ride through the winding streets bordered by trees would be so peaceful in any other situation. Now it felt like the road to nowhere. So much uncertainty and possible danger awaiting them at every turn. Julia still couldn't regret helping Jake. That man would have killed him if she hadn't. As long as he made it through this, it would all be worth it.

Julia looked up at the glimmers of sun coming through the random openings in the branches. The breeze felt good through her hair. She could almost pretend life was normal for a moment. That they weren't constantly running for their lives. That there weren't men who wanted to kill a child. For what? She still had no idea. Maybe if they found the drive, it would provide some answers. Some rationale to all that had happened.

Something flicked against her leg. Julia looked down and saw an old shopping bag shoved between the console and her seat. She slipped it out. It was from a store that no longer existed. It almost felt like a bad omen. She shoved it back down and looked forward.

Troy took a roundabout way to her house. He finally pulled onto her street and rolled to a stop. "I didn't see anyone anywhere. I think I'll be able to keep a better eye on things from the front. That's the more likely place they'd come from at this point. I want you to stay in the Jeep while I take a look around." He parked one door down, across the street from Julia's house. He stepped out onto the pavement, his eyes scanning everything as he moved. "If you see anything, leave. The keys are in the ignition. I'll meet you at the diner if we get separated."

Troy didn't wait for an answer. His steps were barely audible as he headed for the house. He walked along the outer edge of her property and disappeared into the backyard. Jake leaned forward, next to her, resting his arm on the back of the driver's seat. He watched with her, looking eager to get inside. It wasn't long before Troy was walking out her front door. Jake jumped over the side of the Jeep, impatient to get out. Julia followed, stepping through the door.

"Your back door was wide open. No one is here, but they tore the place up. If it was here, I doubt it is now." He came down the front walk, onto the street to meet her. He turned to the house as Jake ran inside then back to her. "I'm guessing that drive is the reason they went after Jake's family. They were definitely looking for something. It's probably gone."

Julia started up the front walk. Her feet were heavy with dread. "I guess there's only one way to find out." This little house, in this little town, had been her sanctuary for the last eight months. She had been experimenting with recipes and trying them out on the locals. She was free of judgment. Free of the anger that had filled her childhood home. Free from the condemnation that still echoed in her mind when things were too quiet, mostly during the night. Now her home was torn apart. Violated. She would have to come to terms with that later.

Stepping inside should have been shocking. Furniture was upended with the cushions torn and scattered about. Walls were marked and dented where wood tables had smacked against them. Her kitchen cabinets had been emptied onto the countertops and floor. Everything she cared about had been tossed aside or broken. Somehow, none of it mattered. Her only concern was the harried panic of Jake's movements as he hurried through the house, picking things up and moving things around, trying to find what his father had died for.

Julia stood in the doorway, thinking back to that night. It felt like a week had gone by. She walked into the laundry room, to the back door, and turned around. She got down on her hands and knees to look under the washer and dryer. She rose and looked carefully into the corners of the room and along the floor. She checked where the kitchen table had been, in the corner where Jake had crouched down while she'd waited to swing the seltzer bottle, and along the floor in front of the bottom cabinets, knowing it wouldn't be in any of those places. Someone had spent time searching already. If it had been here, it was likely gone now.

She walked into the living room, where

Jake was still in a frenzy. Then the sound echoed in her memory. The muffled click of something small hitting the wood floor. She had been putting her sneakers on by the front door. The small entry rug was already thrown across the room, so it wasn't under there. She opened the coat closet door and looked around. Nothing but a mess of shoes. They had been neat, but were now like the rest of her little home. She looked over at Jake, hoping he might have found it. He was putting a chair back on its legs and then he slumped in the seat, defeated. Turning back to the interior of the closet, Julia began pulling the shoes out, one by one, hoping for the impossible. She began tossing the shoes, frustration nearly bringing her to tears.

"You found it!" Jake hollered and ran across the room. She turned to find him kneeling on the floor. He picked up the smallest zip drive she had ever seen. She looked down and realized it had been inside a wooden clog-style shoe. It must have come out when she'd tossed it with the others. Jake threw his arms around her as she stood up, nearly knocking her off her feet. She looked out the front window and saw Troy leaning against the Jeep, watching them. She smiled at him, their eyes passing relief between them.

There was a ticking noise she hadn't noticed before. Had it been there the whole time? Where was it coming from? She listened closely, trying to discern the source of the sound. Following the hollow ticks led her back into the kitchen. It was getting louder. She stood in the center of the room and closed her eyes, focusing on the sound.

Jake moved by her side. "What's wrong?"

Julia turned and opened a lower cabinet. The upper cabinets were already ajar, some barely hanging on by the loose hinges. When she saw nothing, she tried the one next to it. The shock of what she found sent her tumbling backwards onto the floor. There was a device with a clock counting down. And there were mere seconds left before time ran out.

Troy stepped away from the Jeep at the sight of the shift in Julia's expression. What had happened? She'd looked so relieved a moment ago. He had been certain she'd found what she'd been looking for. She and Jake disappeared a moment later. Could someone have gone inside through the back door?

Why wouldn't they drive right up to the front? They couldn't possibly think she would come back here. He wouldn't have brought them if it hadn't been absolutely necessary. He took a step forward when the house blew apart in a ball of fire. Troy's body was thrown back against the Jeep before he dropped to the pavement. Everything went dark.

The sound of sirens pulled him from the murkiness of near unconsciousness. Or had he been out? He couldn't be sure. The ringing in his ears made it difficult to focus. His head spun as though he had been out on rough seas for hours. His stomach lurched with sudden nausea, drawing him up into a seated position and leaning to the side as he almost heaved. An ache radiated throughout his entire body. Trying to right himself, he turned toward Julia's house. It was engulfed in flames. There was no way anyone could have survived that. The entire structure was burning and breaking apart. Pieces of the wreckage were strewn about in the yard and on the street. The heat pressed against his face and chest, forcing him to imagine what it must have been like inside. The creaking and moaning of the fire sank into his bones with an unbearable sadness. He'd failed them. How could he have been so careless?

The sirens moved in, pressing on the throbbing pain in his head, then abruptly stopped. The flashing lights discolored everything around him. A muffled voice pulled his eyes up. Leo. What was he doing there?

"Troy! Are you all right? What happened? Was anyone inside?" Leo helped Troy shuffle back to lean against the front tire of the Jeep. Leo turned and called to someone else. Troy couldn't focus on what he said. All he could do was stare at what was left of Julia's house, knowing he'd lost her. That he would never have the chance to get to know her. The one person who had been able to really see him. She had made him feel something other than broken for the first time in ten years. Another unbearable loss. It was too much.

And Jake. He was so young. So innocent. He'd been through too much. The anguish that filled Troy's veins had him trying to stand. Leo pushed down on his shoulders as another man appeared, dressed in a paramedic's uniform. He was shining a light in Troy's eyes, asking him questions he didn't care to answer. Ignoring him, Troy grabbed onto the Jeep tire and pulled himself to his knees. Leo helped him the rest of the way up.

"He really shouldn't be moving. He should be taken to the ER to have a more thorough exam." The paramedic spoke to Leo as if Troy wasn't there.

"I'm fine. I need to get in there. I need to see if…" He couldn't finish the sentence. He knew there was no hope. He turned to the sky, questioning how this could happen. How a kind woman and an innocent boy could have been taken this way.

"Let the firemen do their job. I'll go in with you when it's safe." Leo held his arm, keeping him steady as his mind slowly came back into focus and his body regained stability.

"Back here!" a man's voice bellowed from behind the burning house. The paramedic grabbed his bag and ran off. Troy was practically on his heels. What had they found?

SEVEN

When Troy came around the corner, into the yard, he saw a paramedic hovering over two figures. He ran without thought and dropped by Julia's side. "Is she alive? Is she breathing?" He didn't give the man a chance to answer. He put his hand on her arm. "Julia, can you hear me? It's Troy. Please open your eyes. I need to see those beautiful eyes." *Please Lord*, he pleaded. The first prayer he had said in years. *Please don't take her from me.*

There was a groan. Jake was opening his eyes. Troy was so grateful, but now he needed Julia to do the same. Two paramedics quickly ushered Jake to the ambulance in the street while the one who'd checked Troy continued working on Julia.

Troy leaned closer. "Julia, please wake up. Open your eyes for me." His voice was barely more than a whisper. Her face had a little scrape and her clothes were dirty, but she didn't appear to have any broken bones or life-threatening lacerations. She almost looked as if she could be sleeping, but she was too still.

He felt a hand on his shoulder. He looked up and saw his old friend, Leo. "How is she?"

Troy shook his head. "I don't know." He held Julia's limp hand in his, begging God for help. The paramedic told him that her vitals were good, but they wouldn't know anything until they ran tests, and he wanted to move her into the ambulance. Troy gently put her hand down so he could get out of the way, as much as he didn't want to, when her eyes fluttered open.

"Troy?" Her voice was weak but she knew who he was. That was a good sign, wasn't it? "Where's Jake? Is he okay?"

Troy felt an overwhelming sense of gratitude he had never experienced before. He found himself whispering, "Thank you." It was directed at God. This was the first time in a very long time that he felt he had something to be grateful for. "He's going to be fine. The paramedics are taking care of him right now. They need to do the same for you. I'm so glad to see you awake, Julia. Now let them take care of you." He started to move when she grabbed his hand. Then he felt something small slip into his palm. She didn't say a word about it. Only made brief eye contact before closing her eyes again.

Troy closed his fingers around the drive and stood up. He then casually put his hands in his pockets and let it drop inside. He kept his hands there for a minute, as if it were part of a contemplative moment. There was no telling who around them could have a connection to the men pursuing this little device.

Once Julia was rolled away, Leo came closer. "I'm glad your friend is all right. I'll need to ask her and the boy some questions when they're feeling up to it. What happened here?"

Troy shrugged. "I'm not really sure. One minute, I was looking at them walk away from the front window. The next, the house blew apart and threw me like a rag doll. I think I may have been knocked out." Troy considered telling Leo about the drive, but decided to hold off. He didn't want his friend drawn into this any more than was necessary. If Leo knew about it, he'd want to see it. Given the lengths these people had gone to, and the possibility that some of the cops were a part of it, he couldn't risk his friend's life. They had already killed a cop to protect their secrets. Troy knew there was no stopping Leo from investigating, but if he didn't know too much, maybe no harm would come to him.

"Jake may be my only witness to identify the players." Leo's expression looked grave.

"Did his mother…"

"No. No, nothing like that. She's awake. They think she'll be all right. One of my guys just spoke to her. She has no memory of that night or several days leading up to it. They had to tell her about her husband. You can imagine how that went." Leo never liked having to give someone bad news about a loved one. "She's asking to see Jake. I'm not even sure what to tell her."

"I don't want to bring him there. I need to take him somewhere safe. Where no one will think to look for him. I hate to tell you this, but I saw one of your guys going around town asking about them. Unless you put him up to it…?" Troy was hoping that was the case.

Leo shook his head. "Not me." He ran his

hands down his face. "I can't believe this is happening here. So, I've got dirty cops on my force. Do you know who it was?"

Troy only knew a few of them. "Not this one. I only knew because of his uniform." He gave a general description of the man he'd seen. "So, you can see why I need to keep them with me for now. I'm hoping they'll be well enough to skip the ER. I don't imagine they'd make it out of there alive."

"If the medic will clear them, I've got a place you can lay low for a while. It's a little hunting cabin I rent sometimes. It's vacant now. I know the owner. He's been complaining that things have been slow and no one has booked it in a while. I know where he hides a spare key."

"You don't want to run it by him first?" Troy didn't like the idea of squatting in someone's house without permission. But, then again, anyone could be a part of this.

"No. The fewer that know, the better. Let's keep the circle small. The last thing I want is for harm to come to anyone else. You go check in with them while I talk to the fire marshal to get a better sense of what happened here." Leo walked toward a man standing at the side of the house, waiting for him.

Troy went out to the street where Julia and Jake were sitting up in the back of an ambulance. They both looked considerably better. They weren't as pale as they'd been when they were first waking up. As he approached, one of the paramedics stepped in front of him.

"They're refusing to go to the hospital. Maybe you can talk some sense into them."

"Is it absolutely necessary? Do you think they have anything seriously wrong?" Troy looked to Julia then back to the man in front of him.

"Honestly, I think they're both fine. It's more of a precaution. The woman took the brunt of the blow. From what they've said, they saw the bomb in a kitchen cabinet and ran out the back door. The woman shielded the boy. I think something from the house hit her in the head, but everything is looking as it should now. Her vitals are normal. Maybe a mild concussion, like you. I guess you're both stubborn." The man shook his head, his mop of dirty-blond hair falling in his eyes. "Keep an eye on each other. Come in if there's any question."

"I will definitely do that." Troy went to Julia and Jake. He couldn't help but pull them both in close. The relief he felt relaxed some of the tension in his body. "I can't even begin to tell you how relieved I am to see you both sitting here like this. I thought you were gone." He pulled Julia tighter against him. "We need to go. There's too much activity here. The sooner we leave, the better our chances of not being followed." He helped each of them step down.

Julia looked at her house with anger in her eyes. This was similar to the morning he'd met her, but without the fear. He would have thought she'd be a shivering mess. Mostly, she looked furious. "They blew up my house." Her voice was low. "They nearly killed Jake. Again. They have to be stopped before they do any more harm."

"They will. For now, I need to get you out of here." He quickly ushered them back to the Jeep and helped them in, making sure their seat belts were fastened. He noticed Julia still staring at her house and the activity around it.

Troy started driving through the maze of emergency vehicles and saw Leo talking to some people. They passed a look between them and Leo nodded and pulled out his cell phone. Then Troy noticed one of the men standing there with him in a police uniform.

It was the cop he'd seen on Henry's farm this morning. Their eyes locked and the man took a step closer to them, but stopped, likely realizing there were too many people around. Troy hit the gas the moment he cleared the emergency workers and spectators who had gathered up the street. He checked the rearview mirror every few seconds on the way out. That cop was trying to get to his car, but kept being held up. That would give Troy more time to get out of sight.

A text came in from Leo with the location of the cabin. He had Julia type back that the cop Leo was talking to when they'd driven by was the one he'd seen asking around about them.

"That was him? From this morning?" Julia's eyes were wide.

Troy nodded. "I wasn't sure at first. But the way he was eyeing me. It was him."

A text came in from Leo.

Are you sure?

He had Julia answer.

100%

Leo then responded.

I'll start digging into him. Get to the cabin. Stay out of town for now. I'll bring you supplies in the morning.

Julia put the phone down. "What cabin?"

Troy glanced at her. "Leo knows of an empty cabin we can hide in for a while." He turned back to Jake. "Leo said your mom is doing better. She's awake, but she doesn't remember anything that happened. Maybe you can give her a call when we get to the cabin."

"I want to see her." The kid looked sad. How much more would he be put through?

"I'm sorry, buddy. It's not safe to do that right now. Not for you or your mom. I promise to get you there as soon as possible. We don't want to put her at risk while she's trying to get better, do we?" Troy tried to be gentle about it. Nothing about this situation was fit for a child. Hopefully, his mother would pull through.

"I guess not." Jake sighed and let his head fall back against the seat. If only there was a way to hide them both while Troy investigated. He'd be able to move more freely that way. There was just no way to be sure they wouldn't be found.

He turned to Julia. "At least you got the drive. I don't know when we'll be able to look at it. I doubt there'll be a computer in the cabin. I'll figure something out tomorrow. For now, I think we need to get out of sight and the two of you need to rest."

Julia nodded. "I wish we could see what's on it now. It could hold answers that will put an end to this. Maybe we can go to your house. Or maybe the library—"

Troy cut her off. "Absolutely not. Look what just happened. My house could have a bomb in it, too. Public places are too risky. We don't know who is involved. We could walk right into someone who's looking for us. Let's take the night to let things calm down and figure it out in the morning." There was no way he would risk anything else happening to them. He could ask Leo to bring a laptop with him in the morning. He would think of a good reason for it. Going forward, the priority was keeping Julia and Jake safe.

The ride to the cabin took them over some rough terrain. Julia held on as the Jeep rocked and bumped up the mountain. She couldn't help but notice the change in Troy's demeanor. He was so warm and affectionate with her and Jake after the explosion. Julia couldn't deny liking the way it felt to be held by him. He had been more stern the last couple of days. Now he seemed more open. More…something she couldn't quite find the words for. She looked over at him. This man had completely turned his life inside out for them. How could she every repay so much kindness?

The image of the rubble left after the explosion shifted her focus. It was probably going to plague her for a while. She had never been so close to death. And it seemed probable that it wouldn't be the last time. That house had been the first one that had ever been just hers. But now that it was gone, she was beginning to realize what it really had been for her. A place to hide from her life. From her parents and everything that reminded her of what she'd walked away from when she'd chosen her own path. She was beginning to realize that she had to rely on God's guidance and not worry about whether others approved. She had always found comfort in Him.

When she'd dropped out of medical school and enrolled in a culinary program, Julia wasn't sure how she would get through it. Her father said so many things, all of which culminated into one simple message. She was going to fail. She realized now that she'd come to Bluerock to try out her new venture because her father wouldn't be there to see when she fell on her face. It had seemed inevitable at the time. Now it all seemed insignificant. Everything that had felt so important, so utterly defining, had been superficial, worldly things. Would her life be over if she didn't succeed in a business venture? No. God would still be there, providing what she really needed. So many years wasted living in fear.

The sound of whining motors pulled her from her reverie. Troy was slowing down and pulling between rows of dense bushes. "We'll stay out of sight until they pass."

Julia looked back at Jake. He had dosed off. She shook his leg and he started. "No going to sleep right now. You have to stay awake for a while." He nodded and she turned back to Troy. "Are you sure we can trust Leo?"

"Of course. He's trying to help. He could have insisted we were brought in for questioning. It would have been easy to have that cop take us in his car and…take care of things. Instead, he gave us a place to hide." Troy dragged a hand through his hair. "I hope this place has running water. I think we could all use a hot shower."

Julia nodded, not wanting to make any sound. The quads were close now. They had just stopped and were turned off. Men's voices could be heard. One of them said something about needing to go to the bathroom, followed by the sound of him traipsing through the dead leaves. He was getting closer. Julia turned back to Jake and waved her hand, signaling for him to get down onto the floor. He moved quickly. A reminder of how much danger he had already seen.

Troy pulled a tarp from behind his seat and covered Jake. The footsteps were getting nearer. Julia sat very still, hoping they wouldn't be spotted. Her mind raced with possibilities and her heart began to hammer against her ribs. Troy pulled her close, face to face, their lips nearly touching, as the man came into view. He stopped, taking them in. She could barely breathe.

"Oh, sorry. Didn't know anyone was out

here. Didn't mean to, uh, interrupt." The man was young, probably a teenager. He turned and left right away. Moments later, the quads started up and moved out of range.

Troy held her there a moment longer, staring into her eyes. Something shifted in his gaze and she froze. Would he lean closer? Would his lips connect with hers? He wouldn't…would he? She couldn't help but wonder what it might be like to kiss him, if only once.

EIGHT

Troy slowly released Julia and moved away. Had he wanted to kiss her? Did he think of her that way? Did she feel anything romantic toward him? All questions that shouldn't be on his mind. His instinct had been to give the impression of a couple sharing an intimate moment to deter the onlooker from making any connection to Jake or the zip drive. Anyone involved knew there was a man and a woman protecting the boy. Covering him up with the tarp and projecting the silly illusion seemed the easiest way to get those young men on their way without incident. He thought he'd even heard them laughing before the engines started back up. He hoped Julia didn't feel disrespected. That wasn't his intention.

The rest of the ride was quiet. Jake was

likely longing to see his mother. Julia's tense expression kept him a little distracted. Not the frame of mind he needed to have now. He pulled himself back into focus. Keeping them safe was his main priority. The emotional stuff could wait, assuming there was even anything to address. Julia may have understood what he was doing. She hadn't pushed him away. Again, he needed to focus. They would arrive at their destination in a matter of minutes. They were still exposed.

The cabin was small but well-kept. The key was in the rock bed, where Leo said it would be, but it didn't fit the front door. He tried a few times before walking around to the back, where he tried again. Fortunately, this door opened. He walked through the cabin, noting the sparseness of the place. There was a small living area with the bare basics of a kitchen. There was one couch, a small table with two chairs, and a wooden chest in the corner. No pictures. The curtains were solid green and were hung on a simple white rod. One door opened into a small bedroom with a queen-sized bed. The other was a small bathroom with a shower stall instead of a tub.

Through the front window, Troy could

see Julia standing with Jake. Even with soot smeared on her face and clothes and streaked through her thick blonde hair, she was beautiful. He stopped for a moment, watching her pull Jake in to comfort him, like Troy's mother had held him as a child. He pushed the thought away and opened the front door.

"It's small, but it's clean." He stepped aside as they walked inside and looked around.

"Any food? I think Jake should eat. It's been hours." Julia walked over to the small cluster of cabinets and started pulling them open. There were plates and cups, but no food. She turned and looked at Troy. "I almost forgot, we can use what Henry gave us."

"I'll grab the cooler." Troy walked outside and got everything Henry gave them. He carried them inside to find Julia holding her hand under the faucet in the kitchen sink.

"We can take hot showers." She smiled up at him.

Troy set everything down on the counter and then Julia took over, putting things away in the refrigerator and getting a meal started. They all took showers and were able to find clothes to wear in the closet. Julia washed what they had been wearing in the kitchen sink, using dish soap, and hung everything on a clothesline out back. She also checked Troy's stitches, then cleaned and covered the wound with the supplies Henry had sent with them. She hadn't said much all day. He worried he may have really offended her when he'd leaned in so close, nearly kissing her. He waited for her to put Jake to bed, later that evening, hoping they could talk.

Julia pulled the door closed as quietly as she could, with the squeaky hinges giving a little moan. "He just dosed off. He really wants to see his mother. I think we should try and find a way to make that happen."

Troy shook his head. "It wouldn't be safe. They could be waiting for us to do that."

Julia sat on the couch, a sigh rushing from her lips. "I know. I tried to tell him, but it's his mother. The last time he saw her was when she was shot in front of him. He needs to see that she's all right with his own eyes. He seems to think your friend would help. He trusts that you wouldn't keep talking to him if you thought he was a threat to us."

Troy sat down next to her, careful not to move too close. He leaned his head back and closed his eyes. "I get it. I'd give anything to see my mother again. And Leo probably would help, but I can't be sure he's trusting the right people." He hadn't meant to say the part about his mother out loud. Something about Julia seemed to make him feel a little too comfortable. Things kept slipping out. He stared up at the wood beams. "I know this is hard on him. All of it. But we can't take unnecessary risks with his life. Better we keep him alive than have to explain to his mother how we lost him."

He felt Julia move closer and put her small hand on his. "This must bring up old wounds for you. A young boy nearly losing his mother. Unknown killers hunting us. I'm sorry you had to get involved in this."

Troy turned his body toward her. "Don't be sorry. I'm glad I left for my run early that morning. I wouldn't want anything to happen to you. I was older than Jake when I lost my mother. I can't deny that I've been remembering things I hadn't thought about in a while, but it's good. I needed to think about her again. To remember all of the things that made her such a great mom. I see some of that in you. You're so good with Jake… You mentioned that no one has ever come through

for you. Not even family. Are your parents…
gone?"

"No, very much alive. They don't approve
of my choices. I haven't spoken to them in a
few years. I haven't had contact with anyone
from home since moving here." Julia looked
so sad at the mention of her parents. Troy
couldn't fathom her mother and father feeling disapproval for her.

"What choices? I can't imagine you doing
anything that would make anyone angry
enough to cut you off." Troy held her hands
between his.

"You haven't met my parents. I was supposed to be a surgeon. Nothing less was ac-
ceptable to them. They have a very specific
set of standards that have absolutely nothing
to do with what I may or may not want to do
with my life. It's been very difficult. They cut
me off financially, too. I never had to support
myself before. It was a little scary, but I really wanted to bake. I was miserable and they
didn't care. So, I gave it all up and took out a
loan. I couldn't do a degree program or go to
the school I would have liked to attend, but I
learned the basics. Then I moved here to ex-
periment. The rent was reasonable and there

were businesses willing to give me a chance. It went better than I'd expected." Julia pulled one hand away and wiped a single tear from the corner of her eye.

"Hey, you did the right thing. And you've done great. I've seen your stuff for sale all over town. And it always sells out. You should be proud of what you've accomplished."

She looked up at him, surprise filling her moist eyes. "But I lost my family. I walked away from them and I didn't go back. I was a coward."

Troy edged closer. "No, you were very brave. Most people in that position would have stayed and done what their parents said. They wouldn't have risked so much to go after a dream with no safety net. You can always reach out to them, when you're ready. Not that they would deserve it."

Her gaze dropped. "Thank you for saying that. Maybe when this is over, I'll get in touch. What do I have to lose, right?" Her eyes lifted to meet his. "If they still don't want me, I haven't lost anything more and I'll know I tried. The funny thing is, when I was running through the woods and that man yelled for me to stop, and he pointed that gun at me,

I was sure that was it. I was going to die. I was terrified for Jake. He's so young. But I also wondered if my parents would care that I was gone. If they would regret any of it. Or if they would pretend I never existed. Like they do now."

Troy pulled her close, wrapping his arms around her little body. "I'm sure they would care. People get angry and say the wrong things. They don't always know how to take it back. There is no doubt in my mind that they would regret all of it if something happened to you."

Julia inched back, her eyes wet with tears. Troy wiped them away. She stared up at him, so open and gentle. He began to feel drawn to her. He was nearly as close as he'd been in the Jeep earlier, before he'd realized what he was doing. He pulled his head back.

"I'm sorry. I didn't mean to disrespect you. Not now or earlier."

Her eyebrows knit together and her head tilted slightly to the side. "Disrespect me? How do you mean?"

"I got too close earlier. I was trying to make that guy leave and it was the first thing

I thought of. If they thought we were a couple… I figured they would go."

She shifted uncomfortably, her eyes turning down again. "I understood what you were doing. I didn't feel disrespected." Her voice was barely louder than a whisper.

Troy inched away. "It's getting chilly in here." He put his arm around her, rubbing her shoulder to warm her. "It gets colder up here at night than in town. Are there enough blankets for Jake?" He nodded in the direction of the bedroom.

"I think so. I'll go check on him." She stood up and walked to the bedroom door, carefully opening it to keep the noise down. She glanced back at him with a hint of an adorable smile before slipping inside.

Troy sat back, considering the smile. Maybe she hadn't been offended. Did she want him to kiss her? What was it about her that seemed to constantly draw him in? To finally feel a real connection to another person? He had been very careful to keep everyone at a safe distance for a long time. Now he felt a strong desire to be close to her. To really know her. How could anyone turn their back on her? Her parents must have been fools to abandon her that way.

* * *

Julia took another blanket from the closet and covered Jake with it. She watched him sleep, his soft snores making it easy to forget the situation they were in. He looked so innocent tucked in that bed. She would miss him when this was over. Almost as much as she would miss Troy. She didn't have a house to go back to and there weren't many rentals in Bluerock.

She touched her fingers to her lips, still buzzing from the possibility of a kiss. Troy was unlike anyone she had ever met. She trusted him in a way she'd never thought possible. Maybe a kiss wasn't the best idea. It would only make her feel the kind of attachment she had successfully avoided most of her life. Growing up in a home where she always felt like a disappointment had made it difficult to let people in. It was easier to keep everyone at a distance so they couldn't hurt her. God was all she needed. He was there for her no matter what. The people in her life were less reliable. But spending time with Troy made her question if she should have tried to let others in. He was proof that not everyone was like the people who raised her.

Troy stepped into the doorway, his form a dark shadow. He whispered, "Is everything all right in here?"

Julia crossed the room and led him back out to the living area, closing the door behind them. "I put another blanket on him, just in case."

"I found another one in the chest in the corner. You can use it on the couch."

Julia shook her head. "What about you?"

Troy guided her onto the couch and pulled the blanket over her. He leaned over and kissed her forehead. "I'll be fine. I've slept in much worse places overseas. You need rest. You were in an explosion today. You shouldn't have to sleep sitting up. I want to keep watch for a while anyway." His intense blue eyes met her gaze with a warm smile before he stepped away.

Julia watched Troy walk over to the window and lean against the frame. His large, muscular build looked even bigger in this small space. How long would he stand there? Her eyelids were beginning to feel heavy. Maybe a little rest would be good.

Julia slipped in and out of sleep throughout the night. The couch was a little lumpy and it was difficult not to wake from every little noise. Sleep had never come easy to her. The night was when she had always been alone with her thoughts. And sometimes, it was the time her father liked to let her know his thoughts about her. How she had embarrassed him on a given day. How she wasn't measuring up to some standard that continually changed with his moods. Sometimes he would take his bad day out on her, inventing reasons to scold her.

Even after so much time away from home, Julia still hadn't been able to sleep through the night. Some were worse than others, but the early signs of the rising sun always seemed to settle her mind. Maybe because her father was busy with work during the day and that was the time that felt safe to her. Her current circumstances certainly didn't make sleeping any easier.

When the first hint of light began to cut through the darkness, Julia felt her body begin to settle in. She noticed that Troy had dosed off, sitting with his back against the front door. She was relieved that he was finally getting some rest. She slipped into a deep sleep, her dreams a mix of fear and the happiness she felt to have met Troy. Then there was something else. A voice trying to pull her out. A grip on her arm that brought her back to the woods as she tried to get away from that man to help Jake. The fear was consuming her. The anguish making her feel helpless. Then there was the feeling of warm light and she felt jostled. Her body jolted and her eyes flew open as she realized what those words had been.

"Someone's here."

NINE

It was barely more than a whisper. Jake was crouched beside Julia, pulling on her arm. His eyes were wild with fear. Julia sat up, her heart nearly leaping from her chest.

"Who's here?" She spoke in a whisper as she got up and moved quietly to Troy's side, where he was still sleeping against the front door.

"I saw a police car. We have to go." Jake's loud whisper was enough to wake Troy. He opened his eyes and, seeing their expressions, jumped to his feet and looked out the window, being careful not to move the curtain.

"It's Leo. We're fine. He's on our side. I promise." Troy reached for the handle.

"He's not here alone." Jake grabbed Julia's arm and pulled her toward the bedroom. "We need to hide."

Julia followed, knowing Jake was too young to understand that not all police were bad. It was easier to make him feel safe if she went with him while Troy spoke to his friend. "We'll be in the bedroom. Come get us when he leaves."

"He'll probably have questions for both of you. A lot happened before I got involved. The more information he has, the better his chances of shutting these guys down before it goes any further." Troy started when someone rapped hard on the door. Two sharp knocks and then nothing. He reached for the handle. "I'll see what he says and then I'll decide whether to let him talk to you."

Julia nodded and closed the bedroom door. Jake ran to each of the two windows, looking frantically in every direction. "I don't know where that guy went. I saw him looking around before they came to the door. He might still be out there."

Julia walked to the window and glanced around. Everything was quiet. "Are you sure they were together?"

Jake didn't answer. They could hear men's voices in the other room. Troy was asking Leo who he'd brought with him.

They should have left town. This felt off. Too close. What if all of the police in Bluerock had been compromised? What if Troy had been wrong about his friend?

"He hasn't told me anything else. It's been tense around here. The kid doesn't trust anyone. Can you blame him?" Troy was hoping Leo would come with some answers this morning. He'd brought breakfast sandwiches and pancakes from the diner, but he was looking for information and Troy didn't have any.

"Maybe I should talk to the boy. I've met him. His father knew me. Maybe he'll open up to me. I'm not a complete stranger. Or maybe the woman. Julia, right?" Leo walked deeper into the room and put the bag of food on the counter.

"I don't know. They're both very cautious right now. I think it'd be better if I speak to them and let you know what I find out. I was really hoping you'd have some news. Something that would put an end to it all." Troy wrapped his hand around the doorknob, feeling protective of the people inside. He trusted Leo, but he had become attached to Julia and felt a sense of responsibility for both of them.

And he wouldn't risk damaging their trust in him again.

"I have an update on Jake's mom. Maybe he'd talk to me to hear about that. His mom gave me a message for him. She's awfully worried, not being able to see him." Leo leaned back against the counter and crossed his arms. Something he always did when he was about to dig his heels in.

"I can certainly ask him, assuming they're back." Troy slowly turned the knob. "They went out for a walk this morning and I dosed off. You woke me up. I'm not even sure if they're here. I'll check." Why was he hedging with Leo? He couldn't let Jake's uncertainty about everyone cloud his judgment. And Leo had to know Troy would never let them go anywhere without him.

He slipped inside and looked around, only to find that the room was empty. Were they in the closet or under the bed? Why were they hiding? "Julia? Jake?" There was no response. He dropped down and looked under the bed and found nothing but dust bunnies. The closet was empty, aside from a few jackets and sweatshirts. His throat constricted as his heart bounced wildly in his chest. He glanced up and saw that one of the windows was wide open and the screen had been pushed out. Had they left? Or had they been taken?

Troy ran over and leaned out the open window. The screen was on the ground below. There were no signs of Julia or Jake. No sounds to indicate what direction they may have gone. His stomach knotted. They couldn't be out there on their own. What if someone took them? What if he never saw them again? He ran out into the living area.

"Who did you bring up here with you?" Troy wasn't used to feeling panicked. Keeping an even keel hadn't ever been a challenge before.

"No one. Why?" Leo pushed off the counter.

"Jake said you weren't alone. Who else is out there?" Troy ran to the front door.

"I thought you said they weren't here… Hey, what's going on?" Leo was right on Troy's heels as he ran outside and looked around. "Why are you lying to me, Troy? Please tell me you don't think I'm involved in what happened to that boy's parents."

Troy scanned the area. "Of course not. But why would he think there was someone else here? Were you looking around?" Troy turned to Leo, wanting to see his expression as he answered. Troy was usually pretty good at picking up on a liar.

"Of course, I looked around. I wanted to make sure you were secure. C'mon. What's going on here? Why are you questioning me like this?" Leo stepped closer. He looked hurt.

"I'm sorry. Things have been weird. We have to find them." Troy realized the Jeep wasn't tucked by the side of the cabin. It was gone. He had purposely parked it there so they could get away without much noise if they needed to. It had been facing downhill. They could have put it in Neutral and rolled a ways before turning it on. Did Julia take it? Did someone else take it with them in it? Maybe Julia still didn't trust him after he'd called Leo. Maybe she had been waiting for her chance to take off.

"Let's look around. I can get a few guys up here with dogs. We'll find them." Leo put his hand on Troy's shoulder. He knew it was meant to be comforting, but it wasn't helping.

"The Jeep is gone. Either they took it or someone took them in it." Troy ran his hands through his hair and grabbed the sides of his head. He wasn't used to feeling helpless. His eyes moved rapidly around, hoping to see something. Anything. Their clothes were missing from the line, but Troy's were still there. They'd taken them and left. He felt a small bit of relief, but mostly a sense of betrayal. He had risked his life for them over and over. How could they not trust him?

"Get in my cruiser. They couldn't have gotten far. I haven't been here that long. We'll catch up to them." Leo walked to his car and got in.

Troy stood for a moment and then grabbed his own clothes and followed. What choice did he have? He wasn't going to get anywhere fast enough on foot. If Leo hadn't come, would they still be gone? Would they have snuck off while he'd slept? What would he do if something happened to them?

It was torture trying to remain calm while Leo drove slowly down the mountain. The terrain wasn't smooth enough to go fast. Especially in a regular car.

Leo cleared his throat. "Tell me what you need. I'm willing to help, if you'll let me. If we don't come across them here, where do you want me to look first?"

Troy scrubbed his hands down his face. "I have no idea. I've only known them a few days. And they don't fully trust me. Julia keeps telling me that Jake isn't opening up to her, but I don't know if that's true or if she's still trying to decide if I'm safe to confide in."

He rubbed his eyes. "I've never dealt with anything like this. With the SEALs, we got a target, we made a plan, and we executed the plan. We never had this kind of uncertainty. Things always went wrong and we had to adapt, but we all worked toward the same goal. I never had to worry that my teammates had a separate agenda."

"You're not dealing with trained soldiers. It's a kid and a woman who bakes. They have no idea what they're doing. Cut them some slack. I'm sure they have their reasons. And I'm sure they'll explain when we find them."

"I know. You're right. Take me to my house. I'll get my truck. I'll go wherever I can think of and you can keep your eyes open while you go through your day. I think we'll cover more ground if we split up. I might know of a few places to check. Do you know where Jake might go?" Troy looked over at

Leo, hoping his past interactions with the boy and his father might be helpful now.

"I can check some places I know his father went. The boy might look to go somewhere familiar. Are you sure you don't want to stick together? It might be helpful to bounce ideas off me." Leo pulled onto a paved road, finally able to hit the gas.

"No. Drop me at my house. If I find them, it'll be better if I'm alone. They may feel threatened otherwise." Troy was growing impatient. He wanted to get his truck and start looking. Maybe they'd even be waiting at his house. He wondered if Julia would go back to Henry's farm. They could hide there until he found them. Where else would they go? He should have asked more questions. Gotten to know them better. He had been so focused on finding out what Jake knew, he hadn't inquired about anything else.

Please Lord, keep them safe.

Leo pulled into Troy's driveway and he nearly jumped out before the car stopped moving. Then he remembered what had happened to Julia's house. He would have to check the place before he did anything else. He needed his truck. It was already packed with supplies.

"Hey, keep in touch. I'll do the same. If I see them, should I approach or call you?" Leo leaned over so he could see Troy as he spoke.

"Don't let them out of your sight, but call me. If you have to approach, do it. Otherwise, wait for me." When Leo nodded, he closed the door and ran inside.

The doors had been left unlocked by whomever had been there, but they hadn't torn it apart like Julia's house. Some things had been moved, but everything was still upright and nothing was broken or torn. It was a relief, but seemed odd. He didn't have time to consider the intentions of killers.

After doing a thorough check for any bombs, he decided to change his clothes and splash water on his face. Then he grabbed his keys from a kitchen drawer and went to the garage. He did a quick check, making sure there weren't any bombs or tracking devices in his SUV. The truck was still full of supplies and appeared to have been untouched. That didn't stop Troy from opening everything and doing a thorough inspection. Once he was satisfied, he hit the garage door opener and pulled out. Now he had to decide where to begin his search.

Driving down his road, he felt an odd sense of being watched. It sent a shiver through his body. Was someone there waiting for him to show up, hoping Jake would be with him? Would they follow him now, hoping Troy would lead them to the boy? He looked in his rearview mirror, but no one was there. Maybe he was becoming paranoid after everything he'd seen and heard. This wasn't the type of terrain he was used to in combat.

Julia's house was nothing more than a pile of rubble. Even if they had come there, they wouldn't have stayed. They couldn't hide and there was nothing left they could use. Even her car had been destroyed by the explosion. He continued down the road. Then he remembered telling Julia to meet him at the diner if anything happened while he was checking the house. He clearly hadn't done such a bang-up job with that.

He drove through town and pulled up in front of the small parking lot for the diner. The Jeep wasn't there. He edged along, hoping to see them hiding somewhere around the building. Then that cop who had been looking for them at Henry's farm came walking out. He wasn't in uniform, but there was no mistaking him. He had an athletic build, dark blond hair, and eyes that were so light, it was difficult to be sure of the color at this distance. He was an attractive man, but had something menacing about him. In most ways, he could have blended in with a crowd. But those eyes were hard to miss.

The cop didn't notice Troy at first. Then he looked up and their eyes met. The man froze, his glare unwavering. Something flickered there. What was it? Anger? A desire to act out? Frustration that he couldn't with so many witnesses around?

Troy didn't wait to see what the cop would do. He hit the gas and got out of there before the cop could get to his car and follow. He shouldn't have had his windows down. Now that cop knew what he was driving. And he also knew that he wasn't with Julia and Jake anymore.

Troy hadn't gotten far when a pickup approached quickly, moving close behind him. The sky was gray, threatening rain, making it difficult to see through the reflection of storm clouds on the windshield. The truck moved closer. Troy accelerated. The pickup kept up. Maybe it was a good thing Julia had taken Jake and run. Whatever was about to happen, at least they wouldn't get hurt. He just had to get through this so he could find them. *Lord, keep them safe while I'm not with them... Please help me so I can get to them before someone else does.* Troy hoped his prayers weren't in vain. Whoever was behind him wasn't going to wait much longer before making a move.

A horn blared and the truck started moving along the shoulder to his right.

Troy looked over and saw the blond cop in the driver's seat. His glare was still ice-cold. He was signaling for Troy to pull over, pointing to the narrowing shoulder of the road ahead. When Troy didn't do it, the driver swerved at him. The harsh clash of metal left his ears ringing. Then the two trucks went into a spin, headed directly for a drop-off on the side of the road. Troy tried to right his SUV, but the two vehicles, locked together, were sliding toward certain death.

TEN

Julia slipped into an empty office, keeping Jake close, hoping to go unnoticed by the flurry of hospital staff moving purposefully all around them. She closed the door as quietly as she could. The woman who'd left to use the bathroom wasn't likely to be gone long. After slipping away from the cabin, Jake had convinced her to let him see his mother before leaving town. Julia had formulated a plan on the way down the mountain, only to be detoured by Jake's need to see that his mom was really going to be all right. She had been very careful, coming in through a service entrance on a loading dock, and avoiding the main lobby and most of the parking lot.

The computer on the desk had been left on, the user still logged in. After using it to find out which room Jake's mother occupied, she found a white jacket that belonged to the doctor who had been sitting in this office. Julia put it on, taking note that it was bigger than she'd expected. She buttoned it closed and walked out as though she belonged there, only to pass the doctor on her way back to her office. Julia grabbed a wheelchair that had been left by the nurses' station and had Jake sit in it as though he was a patient. When she passed an empty room on the way to the elevator, she grabbed a blanket off the bed then draped it over his legs and pulled it up to his chin.

Once inside an empty elevator, Julia's tension eased, which quickly became a gasp when a man wearing a uniform and a badge jutted his arm between the doors and stepped inside. She knew it had been a risk to come. The man turned and smiled at her with a friendly nod. That was when she realized he was hospital security, not a Bluerock policeman. He got off on the next floor without a glance back.

Jake looked up at her. "We can't stay here, can we?"

"Not for long, no. We'll check on your mom and then we have to go. I need to get you far away from here." Julia watched the numbers change until the doors finally opened to their floor.

Julia pushed Jake along the hallway, checking the room numbers until she finally found the right one. As she rolled the wheelchair into the room, Jake jumped up while it was still moving and ran to his mother's side. She was sleeping, so he stood watching her, unsure what to do. Julia came to his side and put her arm around his shoulders. He leaned into her while his eyes scanned the cuts and bruises on his mother's face and arms as she slept.

They were too exposed. It seemed unkind, but Julia put her hand on Jake's mother's arm and gently rocked her. The woman's eyes opened slightly, taking them in. When she saw Jake, her eyes went wide and she tried to sit up.

"Jake! What are you...?"

Julia stepped in front of Jake and spoke in a soft tone. "Please keep your voice down. We don't want to draw attention."

The woman's eyebrows pinched together as she focused on Julia. "Who are you? What are you doing here?"

"My name is Julia. I brought Jake to see

you before we leave town. I know you don't remember what happened, but it's important that you don't tell anyone we were here."

The woman shook her head frantically. "I remember everything. I lied so they wouldn't kill me. I'm helpless in here. The police told me that a man and a woman were taking care of Jake and they hadn't been able to speak with him about what happened yet. I assumed you were keeping him from them. Keeping him safe. Why would you risk coming here?" She glanced around the room. "Wait, where is the military man that's supposed to be with you?"

Jake and Julia glanced at each other. Jake turned to his mother. "We left him behind, Mom. He trusts some of the cops. I made Julia leave him and bring me here. I needed to see you." His eyes filled with tears as he threw himself over his mother.

She wrapped her arms around him and looked up at Julia. "Thank you for taking care of him. You'll have to tell me how you got involved another time. You need to get him out of here. They check on me pretty often." She pulled Jake closer. "I love you, my sweet boy, but you need to go. I can't protect you here. Make sure you get the drive to Adam Hayes. He was your father's DEA contact. Do you remember how Daddy told you how to get in touch with him if anything bad ever happened? You still have the drive, right?"

Jake pulled back and turned to Julia, panicked. "Did you get it back?"

Julia's hands shot up to cover her mouth as she shook her head from side to side. "I wasn't expecting to separate from Troy. I'm so sorry."

"I don't have it, Mom. What are we gonna do? They're gonna kill us." Jake's shoulders shifted up his neck, his chest puffing up and down.

His mother reached for him, grabbing his hand. "Everything is fine. There's another copy." Jake started to calm a little. "Go see Marty Wilcox. Ask him for the drive your dad mailed him. Then get in touch with Adam Hayes. Understand?" His mother was so gentle and loving with him. Julia felt awful having to separate them again.

"I will, Mama. I'll get it and then I'll come and get you out of here." Jake was so brave for a boy so young. Sometimes it was hard to believe he was only ten.

Julia leaned back against the wall, needing to pray. *Lord, please keep this woman safe while we get the help we need. Heal her body so she can be with her son. Give her comfort for the loss of her husband. Please don't allow Jake to lose her. And please protect Troy and help him understand why we left. That we trust and appreciate him, but I didn't want to keep putting him at risk. His friendship with the police chief made him more vulnerable. If you have to take anyone, let it be me. Not any of them.*

"Do you remember where Marty lives?" Jake's mother seemed eager to get them on their way. She must've really felt unsafe there. What a terrible feeling to be trapped by her injuries, surrounded by people she couldn't trust.

Jake nodded his head.

"Good. Now come here and give your mom a hug." Jake draped himself over her again. "Please be safe. Take care of each other. I love you. Now go." She released him and watched as Jake got into the wheelchair and pulled the blanket back on. It was heartbreaking to see the pain they were both in, but there was no choice.

Julia took her hand. "I'm going to look after him. You take care of yourself. Keep faking the memory loss. It's probably what's keeping you safe." Then she pushed Jake out into the hall, his body slumping and his head dropping to the side.

She walked toward the elevator then noticed a police officer standing at the nurses' station talking to one of the women behind the counter. Julia stopped short and pulled the chair backward into a patient's room. There was an elderly man in one of the beds, watching TV.

His voice was gruff. "Did you bring my juice? I've been waiting an hour."

Startled, Julia turned to him. "I came to check what kind of juice you want. Apple or orange?" She tried to fake a calm smile. Jake stood up and rolled the blanket in a ball on the seat of the wheelchair.

"I told the other lady I want pineapple. What's going on in this place? How do I get a lousy glass of juice?" Fortunately, the man was too hoarse to be heard outside the room.

"I'll get it right away." She edged closer to the door, grabbing Jake's hand.

"Hey, is that blanket for me?" He was looking at the one Jake had cast aside.

"Of course." Julia pulled the curtain around the rail, blocking them from the open doorway just as that police officer was walking by. Fortunately, he hadn't looked their way. Jake helped her pull the blanket over the elderly man. Then they stood for a moment while she tried to figure out how they would get out of there without being seen.

"How about my pineapple juice?" The man's voice startled her.

"I'll get it now." She smiled at him and led Jake to the doorway. She peaked out and saw that the corridor was empty, with the exception of a young man rolling a tray carrying various meals and drinks. She wondered if the pineapple juice was on that cart. Julia looked up and down the hallway and found a door to a stairwell close by. She pulled Jake to her side and tried to walk at a normal pace, hoping not to draw any attention.

Once the door closed behind them, they ran down the stairs, their hands gliding along the railing. At the bottom, Julia paused and looked through the slim window into the emergency room. There was a flurry of activity. Paramedics were rolling two men in from outside. There wasn't a clear view of the first one. A doctor stopped the second one to look at him before he was brought the rest of the way in.

Julia's heart skipped into her throat. Troy was on the gurney, his head wrapped with a blood-soaked bandage. Guilt consumed her. If she hadn't left him behind, he would still be unharmed. This had undoubtedly happened while he was searching for them. The knot in her throat threatened to restrict her breathing. She had to make sure he was all right. How would she get to him? How would she protect him, as he had protected her and Jake?

Jake must have seen the tension in her body. He ducked in front of her and looked through the bottom of the glass. A moment later, he jerked back and grabbed her arm, pulling her out of sight. "Stay away from the window." His whisper was almost difficult to hear over the humming of the erratic pulse in her ears.

The door handle moved and the blue of a police uniform filled the lower half of the glass. Julia pulled Jake behind her and looked around for something to use. Anything that would buy her enough time to get him out of there. The handle turned and the door cracked open. The officer was facing away, finishing a conversation. There was nowhere to go but back up. And that would definitely draw his attention.

The sounds of beeping machines and chatter pulled Troy from darkness. Where was he? His eyes weren't focused. The throbbing in his head was like a heavy drumbeat. He blinked a few times, trying to see where he was. What was the last thing he remembered? He'd been looking for Julia and Jake. That blond cop had chased him down. They must have crashed. He wondered if the other man had been injured. Troy had to be in the emergency room. Was the other man here in the hospital, too? Was he dead? He wasn't sure what would be worse.

There was a bright light in his left eye. Then his right. "Can you hear me? You've been in an accident. We're going to run some tests on you. Do you understand what I'm saying?" Troy nodded as the kind doctor's face came into focus. She was older. Her eyes were a clear blue and her hair was mostly gray.

Troy tried to speak but his mouth and

throat were so dry, he couldn't get anything out. How would he find Julia and Jake now? He had to get out of here. He leaned his head to the side, trying to get his bearings, and noticed a familiar face. Officer Green was standing nearby, talking to the paramedic. Troy waved his hand, trying to get his attention. The man came over to him and Troy tried to speak again.

"Call Leo." His voice was barely a whisper.

The cop leaned closer. "Say it again, Troy. Can you tell me what happened?"

"Get Leo. I need to see Leo." That was all he could muster. His body didn't have enough energy to say anything more. His head lobbed to the side as he began to lose consciousness. That's when he saw Julia's beautiful face in the narrow window of a door across the room. Her eyes were panicked. He had to get to her.

Officer Green turned to walk toward Julia.

Troy reached out but fell into darkness.

ELEVEN

Julia took advantage of the officer being distracted and quietly backed away from the door. She sent Jake up the stairs immediately, hoping he hadn't been spotted. Once she felt it was safe, she turned to run up the stairs, but was abruptly pulled back. She turned, shock threading through her insides, to the cop she thought had been preoccupied holding her arm in a death grip. How had she missed the sound of the door opening behind her? She could hear Jake's footsteps moving above. She had made sure to tell him to meet her back at the Jeep if they were separated in the hospital. There was some relief, knowing he was out of harms way.

Jerking her arm back, out of the man's grasp, she tried to behave as though she had no reason to run or be chased. "Excuse me,

Officer. Is there a reason you're grabbing me this way?"

The man stood a moment, staring into her eyes. Was he one of them? Was he trying to determine if she was the woman they were looking for?

"I'm very sorry. I thought you were someone else. My sister is a doctor here and she's been avoiding my calls. I thought you were her." He looked repentant, but there was no way to know for certain. She had found herself capable of lying when it came to survival recently.

Julia eyed the man. "You may want to use a more tactful approach with your sister if you don't want her avoiding you in the future."

"Again, I'm very sorry." He stepped back, out of the stairwell.

Julia watched through the window and saw him walk outside. Tension eased from her body. She looked around and realized Troy had been taken away, likely for an exam and possibly treatment. She opened and closed her fingers, hoping to quell the shaking. Realizing Jake was now on his own, she turned and ran up the stairs, stopping short when she saw him standing by the door to the next floor.

"What are you doing here? You should have run. What if that man had been one of them? I'm not fully convinced that he isn't. You were supposed to go if something like this happened."

"I waited. I could hear everything. I would know if I had to run. It was fine." He shrugged his shoulders.

"Next time, run. Don't wait. Don't look back. I'll find you. Don't put yourself at risk, okay?" Julia pulled him close and kissed the top of his head. "I don't want anything to happen to you." She opened the door and guided him through.

They worked their way to another stairwell and went back down. She had to get to Troy. She had to explain what had happened while he'd been talking to Leo and why she and Jake had left. She hoped Troy still had the drive. If not, they would have to go to that family friend Jake's mother mentioned. Julia really didn't want to involve anyone else if she didn't have to.

At the bottom of the stairs, she looked through the narrow window and saw that they weren't in the ER this time. They walked out into the lobby of Bluerock Hospital. Jake scanned the room, on high alert. None of this was healthy for someone so young. He shouldn't have to be on guard, trying to avoid killers. Jake pointed to a directory and they walked over. Julia found the location of the emergency room and then started in that direction. Jake kept looking all around, turning his head in every direction.

"Try not to do that. You're going to draw attention to us. Try to stay calm." Julia couldn't blame him. Her heart was racing, but she tried to present herself as though it was any ordinary day. They made their way through the various corridors, following the arrows leading to where they wanted to go. It didn't take long to find Troy. Each room had a glass wall along the front, making it easy to see who was inside.

Troy's eyes were closed. He looked so peaceful, aside from the stitched gash on his forehead. Julia pulled the curtain from the sidewall and stretched it along the glass, hoping no one would notice. She moved to his bedside and took his hand in hers. "I'm so sorry. This is all my fault. We shouldn't have left you." *Lord, please let him be all right.*

Jake stood watch, peeking around the edge

of the curtain. "Will he get better?" The boy's sad eyes locked on Troy, focusing on the dried blood on his head and the edge of his hairline.

"I hope so." Julia tried to give a comforting smile, but it was difficult.

Troy stirred a little then opened his eyes. "Julia?"

"What happened to you?" She couldn't help the mix of relief and fear in her tone. She was glad to see him awake, but still worried about how serious his condition might be.

"I'm fine. They already ran a few tests. It's a mild concussion. I'll be out of here in an hour." He smiled at her then winced a little. "Why did you leave?"

The dreaded question. "I'll explain that later. Are you really okay?"

Jake grabbed her hand and pulled her between the curtain and the wall on the side of the room, right behind a chair. Julia hoped whoever he'd seen coming wouldn't notice their feet. There was enough space for them to stand without the fabric touching them, but any movement could make them visible.

"Troy, are you awake?" A man's voice boomed through the room.

"Hey, Leo. Did Officer Green tell you to

come? I told him to call you. Have you found Julia and Jake?" Troy wasn't telling his friend they were there. Had Leo done something that had made Troy doubt him?

"He said you were in a pretty serious wreck with one of my officers. That you almost went over the cliff. What happened? And, no, I haven't seen any sign of them. I was hoping you might know where they went." Julia could hear Leo's heavy footsteps moving closer to Troy.

Jake looked as though he might hyperventilate. He was taking long, slow breaths, trying to keep silent. He jumped when the sound of metal scraping on the linoleum tile echoed in the small space. Then Leo's voice was right there. He had taken the seat in front of them. Julia squeezed Jake's hand, hoping to provide some comfort. There was no way Leo would risk letting them go again. Julia closed her eyes, trying to keep her own breathing steady. She had certainly had plenty of practice maintaining the illusion of calm throughout her childhood.

"That was the cop that was asking around. He tried to run me off the road when I wouldn't pull over. He's definitely a part of this." Troy's tone was insistent. Maybe he did still trust the police chief. Julia imagined Leo was in a tight spot, having to consider the men he worked with, who were a symbol of the law, could be criminals.

"Well, I won't be able to question him any time soon. He's in a lot worse shape than you. The doctors are still running tests on him. Can you give me any ideas where to look? If they did this to you, imagine what could happen to a woman and child." There was a long silence after Leo's statement. Julia began to worry that Troy would tell his friend they were there, believing it would be for their own protection.

"So, how bad is my SUV?"

Leo's tone lightened a little. "Not great. I don't think you'll be driving it any time soon."

Julia could hear Troy blow out a disappointed sigh. "Where did they tow it? I'd like to see for myself."

"I'm pretty sure Dale picked it up. Probably behind his service station. You don't need to be worrying about that now. I'll take you where you need to go." Leo did have a kind voice. Almost jovial. Julia wished she could have the faith in him that Troy did.

* * *

Troy pulled himself up to sit, beginning to get his strength back. He had endured much worse injuries and pressed on during his time as a SEAL. He wasn't about to tell Leo or anyone else where to find Julia and Jake. He would be the one to protect them. Leo didn't deserve his distrust, but Troy knew Leo might still confide in the wrong people.

Leo stood up and moved toward him. "Take it easy. You don't want to move too fast."

"I'm starting to feel close to normal. I could use a bite to eat. Then we can go looking together." He hated lying, but he didn't see any other way.

Leo walked to the doorway. "I'll see if I can get someone to bring you food. Then I'll go and get an update on my officer. I would very much like to question him about what he did." Leo stepped from the room. "I'll be back in a little while. Get some rest."

Troy nodded and waited a minute before getting up and checking to see that he was gone. "You can come out now." He turned and nearly toppled over when Julia threw her arms around him. It wasn't what he'd expected.

"I'm so sorry, Troy." She stepped back and looked at him, inspecting every inch. "Are you really fine?"

"I really am. I can't tell you how happy, and relieved, I am to see both of you. We have to go before he gets back. No way he'll let me go off on my own after what happened. He probably feels responsible." He looked over at Jake. "Did you get to see your mom?"

The boy nodded then wrapped his arms around Troy's waist. "I'm glad you're better." Had he finally won Jake's trust? He hoped so. Troy would do anything to protect this little boy and the beautiful woman who'd somehow pierced the thick armor he had built around his heart. How had she done that?

"Thanks, buddy. We should move. Leo will be back soon." Troy realized Julia was wearing a white doctor's coat and nearly laughed. She was resourceful. He pulled his clothes out of the plastic bag on the counter. Julia and Jake turned and kept watch. He dressed as he spoke. "There's a wheelchair right outside the room. You can probably roll me out of here wearing that." He pulled his hiking shoes on and sat on the edge of the bed to tie them. "Is the Jeep here? It sounds like my truck is trashed."

Julia nodded as she stepped out and pulled the wheelchair in. Troy sat down and casually looked around as she rolled him by the busy nurses and doctors, and out the door, Jake beside them. Once outside, Troy got to his feet and followed them around the side of the building, past a loading dock, to a long dumpster. The Jeep was neatly tucked between a concrete wall and the side of the container. He had to admit, Julia had done well on her own. His body was sore all over, causing him to ache as he climbed into the passenger seat. Jake jumped over the side, into the back seat, and leaned forward to help with the seat belt. Troy didn't need the help, but liked that Jake cared enough to want to. It wasn't something he'd allowed in his life in the last several years. Maybe it was time to make a change.

Julia drove out a back entrance, into a residential neighborhood. "I almost forgot, do you have the drive with you?" She glanced over at Troy then back to the road.

Troy's hand instinctively went to his pants' pocket, which was empty. He had forgotten about it in his rush to find them. He blew out a heavy sigh and his face fell forward. "I hid it back at the cabin. I left without think-ing about anything else when I realized you were gone. I can't believe I was that careless!" He was furious with himself. He had never made so many mistakes before. He was be-ginning to remember why he hadn't allowed emotions to intrude on the way he operated. They made him incompetent.

"It's fine. Jake's mother told us his father gave another copy to a friend here in town. We can go there and get it."

Troy thought on that for a minute. There were too many risks. So many unknowns. He didn't like the idea of going to see anyone new at this point. For all he knew, this man could have been the reason Jake's father had been killed.

"I think we should go back up to the cabin. We don't know that this guy was a real friend or if he's involved."

Julia shook her head. "I don't know if that's a good idea. There was a man outside. He didn't look like a cop, but he was dangerous. I'm not sure if the cabin is safe."

"What guy? Where?" Troy turned toward Julia.

"When Leo came inside and seemed intent

on talking to Jake, we decided to slip out the window and wait for him to leave. We stumbled on someone hiding there. I have no idea if he came with your friend or was there on his own. The man immediately tried to grab Jake, so I picked up a fallen branch and hit him. I think I knocked him out."

Troy was stunned. Julia continued. "He was messy, unshaven, had the look of a criminal. We decided you should be left out of it. You kept putting yourself in danger for us, and I know you trust your friend, but we don't know who we can trust besides you. It didn't seem fair to keep making you choose between us and him. I thought you might be relieved if you didn't have to worry about it anymore."

Troy could tell she actually believed that was possible.

He took her hand in his. "First of all, there is no choice. I'm with you." He looked back at Jake to make sure he knew he was included in that statement. "Second, I was built to be in danger. It's my wheelhouse. There is no relief in the idea of the two of you out there without me in the way of anyone that comes at you." Julia opened her mouth to speak. Troy put a finger up and continued. "Third, if anything happened to either of you, I don't think I'd recover. So, please promise me you won't take off without me again." He looked at Jake, who nodded. Then he focused on Julia.

She pulled to the side of the road and turned to Troy. "I promise, but you can't keep risking your life. We need to get the drive and leave town. You keep getting hurt." She reached up and gently touched the wound on his head.

"I'm fine. This is nothing. Getting away from here for a while is probably a good idea." All he could think about when his SUV was spinning off the road was who would look out for them if he was dead. Maybe some distance was the only way to keep all three of them alive. "Tell me where the other copy is. We can ride over and take a look around. Then we'll decide which seems safer."

"His name is Marty Wilcox. He was a good friend of Jake's father. Jake knows where to find him." Julia started driving again.

"I know Marty. I think we should go see my SUV first. I want to get my backpack. It has things we need. It's sitting in the service station in the middle of town."

Julia nodded. "I know the place." Her eyes lifted to the rearview mirror and she tensed.

"What is it?" Troy turned to see before she had the chance to answer.

A police car was approaching fast.

TWELVE

Troy grabbed the tarp off the floor of the back seat. "Get down."

Jake dropped to his knees and sank down in a fluid motion. Troy pulled the thick stained canvas over him, trying to minimize the appearance of his movements. Hopefully, Jake hadn't been seen. He was still short enough to blend with the back of the passenger seat from a distance.

"Keep facing forward. Try to act normal." Troy could see Julia tensing behind the wheel. He looked in the sideview mirror on the door. The cop car was coming fast. The lights began flashing and then the loud blare of the siren filled the air all around them.

Julia turned to him. "What should I do? We know this thing won't outrun a cop car."

"Pull to the side. We'll figure it out. I'll

try Leo." He pulled his phone out and dialed. "Straight to voice mail."

Julia stopped against the curb. The cop car whizzed by. The driver didn't even look in their direction. Her entire body sank into her seat. She stared ahead as the car disappeared around a curve. Everything felt like a possible threat now. The stress of living this way wasn't getting any easier. Moving to Bluerock was supposed to put an end to those feelings, not give her reasons to be more fearful.

Troy pulled the tarp up and Jake got back into his seat. He put his hand on Julia's shoulder. "Are you all right?"

"Yes." She steadied herself and put the car in Drive. "I'll head to the service station. The sooner we get out of this town, the better."

The ride was quiet. Julia thought about her time in Bluerock and decided she was ready to stop hiding when this situation was over. Bad things could happen anywhere. There was no point in limiting herself anymore. Maybe she would get her own bakery. Or sell her goods in more places. She didn't know exactly what she wanted to do yet, but she was definitely ready to live her life without so many restrictions.

The service station was filled with customers. Julia drove down a side street and parked next to a row of tall bushes, under the shade of a big tree. She unbuckled her seat belt to get out.

"You should stay here. I'll grab my backpack and we'll go. It's better if no one sees you with me. For now, they believe we split up. Why give them any advantages?" Troy got out and pushed the door closed.

Julia settled in her seat. "I guess that makes sense."

"I won't be long." Troy hurried along the sidewalk, in the direction of the service station.

Julia turned to Jake. "How are you doing back there? Are you hungry?"

Jake shrugged his shoulders, which seemed to be his go-to response. "I guess I'm a little hungry." He turned around in his seat, looking down toward Main Street. "I think my mom gets sandwiches at the deli over there." He pointed to a place diagonally across the street from the service station. "Hey, there's Mr. Wilcox."

Julia looked in the direction he was pointing. "The man with the white shirt and dark jeans?" There was another man nearby, but he looked much older than she would have expected.

"Yes, that's him." Jake unbuckled his seat belt. "I can go ask him for the drive."

"Wait a minute. We can't go walking into the middle of town." Julia considered the possibility. Would anyone really have the nerve to grab them with so many people around? Given everything else she'd seen, she couldn't be sure of any limits.

Jake jumped over the side of the Jeep and started waving his hands over his head.

Julia got out. "What are you doing? Someone might see us."

It was too late. Marty Wilcox was walking toward them.

"See, it's fine. No one saw and we can talk to him here, where no one will notice us." Jake smiled at the man approaching. Julia watched him, unsure what to do. She wished Troy would come back. This didn't feel right.

"Jake, what are you doing here?" Marty approached cautiously. "Everyone has been looking for you. I'm so sorry about what happened. Have you been able to see your mom?" As he got closer, Jake ran to him and threw his arms around Marty's waist.

"Are you two out here on your own? We need to get you someplace safe." He took Jake by the hand and walked over to Julia.

She had no idea what she should say. Would it be wise to mention Troy was coming back any moment? Would it be better if Mr. Wilcox didn't know?

He held out his hand. "I'm Martin Wilcox. My friends call me Marty. I've been hoping to meet the brave woman taking care of Jake."

Julia shook his hand. "I'm Julia. We were hoping you might help us..." She was about to ask him about his copy of the drive when he pulled a revolver from the back of his pants.

Jake's eyes widened. "Uncle Marty, what are you doing?"

"Don't do anything stupid. Get in the Jeep. We're leaving." He waved the gun to motion her to go. Julia reached for Jake, but Marty pulled him back and nodded at the Jeep, holding the gun to Jake's head. "Get in." She did as she was told. He climbed into the back seat with Jake and told her to start driving. She did, reluctantly, praying that Troy would be able get to them in time. "Don't try anything or you're both dead. Where's the drive?"

Julia looked at him in the rearview mirror.

Troy was right. Again. "We don't have it. We came back to town to get it. His father hid it."

Marty narrowed his eyes at her in the mirror. Then she noticed Troy walking back from the service station. It was too late. They were already too far down the road for him to catch up. She tried to think of what she could drop on the street to give him a clue. She turned her head and saw Jake curled in the corner. He looked so hurt. The poor boy had trusted this man. His father had put complete faith in him. How could he do this to them?

"Where did he hide it? Don't lie to me. If you're here, you know where it is."

Julia wasn't sure how to answer. She had no intention of giving away the real location of the last remaining evidence. "In his house." She glanced in the mirror again and saw Troy was running after them. She let off the accelerator, giving him a chance to catch up.

"No. We tore that place apart. Nothing there. Hit the gas." Marty's tone was clipped.

Julia had no choice but to drive faster. She didn't want to risk him seeing Troy. He had a gun. Troy was unarmed. "Jake told me about a hiding spot no one knows about."

Marty pulled out his phone and made a

call. "You won't believe who I just ran into… That's right. I've got Jake and the woman… No, they don't have it… They're saying it's in the house… I'll meet you there." He glared at Julia in the rearview mirror. "Let's go get it."

"I don't know how to get there." She watched him narrow his eyes on her again. Then he gave her turn-by-turn directions as they went. Julia glanced around, looking for anything she could use. Then she saw it. The ragged white paper sticking up between the console and the passenger seat. It was a bag she'd noticed when Troy had driven them off Henry's farm. She remembered seeing the word *Home* printed in the center when she'd pulled it out to see what it was. An old bag from an old store that didn't exist anymore. She remembered wondering how many years the Jeep must have been sitting under the tarp in that barn.

She dropped her arm casually across the console and let her fingers latch onto the edge of the bag. How would she do this? She glanced at the mirror and saw that Marty was looking at his phone. She used her fingers to slide the bag up onto the passenger seat, then tilted it up and let the wind take it over the seat and right by Marty's head.

He looked up and glared at her again. "What was that?"

"I think it was an old bag. The wind must have rattled it loose." She tried to keep her voice from cracking. The man was holding a gun to the back of her seat. Jake was cowering in the corner. None of this should have been happening. They were supposed to leave town. Get away from all of this madness.

"Drive faster. Stop trying to slow down." He was paying attention, leaving Julia no way to delay the inevitable. What would happen once Marty realized the drive wasn't in that house? An acidic bile crept up her throat.

Their only hope was that Troy would find the bag, remember seeing it in the Jeep, get the message that she'd intended, and find them. Not exactly a stellar plan. Julia sighed into a thick swallow. The air began to feel thin. How foolish she had been to believe they were going to make it out of this. That she had a future. That Jake would be with his mother again. That she would have a chance to really get to know Troy. Her head jolted slightly in surprise. Was that something she wanted? What did it even matter? She and Jake would be dead within the hour. Troy wasn't going to find them that quickly. All she could do was hope he would be left alone once they were gone.

Jake's house was like most of the others in Bluerock. A small center-hall Colonial with a single-car garage. The driveway only held one car. Julia wondered if it belonged to Jake's parents. She pulled up to the curb out front and stopped. She held the brake, hoping for any opening to leave.

Jake jumped over the side and Marty went immediately after him. He grabbed Jake and turned, holding the gun to his neck.

"Turn it off and get out." Marty watched, sliding the muzzle up to the side of Jake's head.

She had no choice. She did as she was told and walked around to the slim sidewalk to meet them. Where were the neighbors? Why wasn't anyone outside to see this? Would someone look out the window and call for help? Why did it seem like no one was ever around when these things happened?

Marty waived the gun, prompting her to walk toward the house. He followed, pulling Jake along. Julia stopped at the front door.

"It's open." Marty's impatience was putting an edge in his voice.

Julia turned the knob and pushed the door, letting it bounce against the inside wall. Her heart began to thump, her throat tightened, and her head felt hazy. She knew someone had been beaten and murdered here. Jake was going to be forced to relive what he'd seen. Why hadn't she thought of something else? And what would she do when Marty and whoever else was coming realized that the drive wasn't really there? Her eyes filled with unshed tears as she tried to keep from letting her body shake uncontrollably. She glanced back and saw Jake's eyes drooping with pain. He was taking quick shallow breaths, barely able to walk. Marty shoved him forward.

"Get it. Now." He gave Jake another push.

Julia stepped in front of Jake. "He shouldn't have to go back in there. He told me where to find it. Leave him here and take me to his father's office. I'll show you where it is." She looked at Jake, waiting for him to lift his eyes to hers, but he was too lost in his grief. She needed him to remember what to do.

Marty glared at her and then at Jake, who had slumped against the wall. "Fine." He grabbed her arm. "Don't go anywhere, kid. If you do, I'll find you once I'm done with her." Jake nodded his head so slightly it was almost unnoticeable. Marty's tight grip was painful. As if he liked the idea of causing pain because he could. He had a gun. There was no need to touch her, let alone hurt her. The gun was more than enough to force compliance.

Julia tried to glance back at Jake, but Marty shoved her up the stairs. Every step felt like she was moving a little closer to her death. At least Jake had a chance now. She just hoped that the pain of being back in this house wasn't clouding his mind. He had to get away before anyone else came. She had made him promise to run if anything like this happened. That he shouldn't worry about her. As they reached the top of the stairs, Julia thought she heard the front door click closed. She prayed Jake would find safety.

Troy ran down the street and turned in the same direction he saw them go. Marty Wilcox had been in the back seat. He had to be a part of this. There was no other explanation for them leaving without Troy. Julia had promised she wouldn't do that again and he believed she meant it. Now he had to figure out where they went. Up ahead, there was an old white bag lying in the street. Why was it familiar? He stopped and picked it up. It was from an old store that had gone out of business at least ten years ago. The bag was yellowed from age. Where had it come from?

Then he remembered the white paper bag Julia had pulled out in the Jeep. Could this be the same one? Had Julia left it behind to help him find her? If she had, what could it possibly mean? He wouldn't know if one of those stores had ever been located in Bluerock. If it had been, he wouldn't know where. He kept moving, but glanced at the bag again. *Home* was printed across the middle of the logo. Were they going back to her house? Doubtful, given that it was little more than a pile of rubble.

He kept moving down the street, until he came to a crossroad. There was no way of knowing which direction Marty had forced Julia to drive. He stood a moment, turning in all three directions. *Home*. Would they have gone back to Troy's house? Marty was probably demanding the zip drive. Maybe Julia had told him they'd hid it somewhere to buy time. His house made sense. He turned left and started in that direction. The afternoon sun was beginning its descent, the breeze carrying cooler air.

Troy looked around as he jogged along, keeping his pace fast and steady, noticing how peaceful it seemed. Neatly-kept homes were nestled along streets lined with mature trees. The sky had cleared and was filling with the reds and oranges of the sunset. The roads were beginning to fill with evening commuters heading home to have dinner with their families. It didn't seem possible that he was running to stop killers from doing unthinkable things to innocent people. Not in a place like this.

Keeping vigilant, he looked into each car, watching to see if the driver took any interest in him. He didn't know many people, so most of them didn't pay him any mind. Occasionally, one would smile and wave to be friendly. He gave a quick wave and kept going.

As he turned the corner, onto his street, he saw Jake running toward his house. Troy sprinted, his backpack slamming against his spine. He wanted to call out, but wouldn't risk drawing attention to the boy. Where was Julia? Why wasn't she with him? As Jake reached the front door, he turned and looked around. His eyes filled with panic, then recognition. He ran toward Troy and met him on the street, just beyond the lawn.

The boy was breathless. He had clearly been running for a while. "We have to go… She needs you." Jake pulled Troy's arm. "We have to go!"

Troy barely understood his jumbled words. "Stop. Catch your breath."

"No time. Julia tricked Mr. Wilcox so I could get away. He had a gun. They're at my house." His voice was still choppy from exertion, but Troy understood that time.

"Show me." Troy followed Jake as he ran through the streets. He wasn't sure how the kid kept going. He was nearly tripping over his own feet he was so tired.

Troy pulled Jake to a stop when they turned a corner and saw the Jeep parked up the road. "Is that your house?" He guided the boy closer to a dense bush, hoping not to be noticed.

Jake was too winded to speak. He nodded and tried to point at his house. His hand was shaking and his arm was dropping. There were two other cars parked across the street.

One was a Bluerock police car. The other was a new, black Camaro with tinted windows. It was impossible to see if anyone was inside.

Troy looked around. "I'm going in there to help Julia. I need you to hide here for me." He pointed to the bush. There was a wood-slatted fence behind it. "Tuck yourself in there until I get back." Troy pulled off his backpack. He unzipped it, pulled out a handgun and a business card. "If we don't make it out, wait until it's completely dark and then call this number. My phone is in the front pocket. Tell Todd I told you to call and that you need his help. You can trust him." Troy tucked the gun into the back of his waistband.

"Keep my backpack with you." He watched Jake squeeze himself between the fence and the outer branches. "There're energy bars and water in there. Take what you want. But stay quiet and out of sight. Got it?" When Jake nodded, Troy started moving along the rear perimeter of the house next to Jake's. He kept low in front of the windows and made his way into Jake's yard. As he pressed himself against the outer wall, next to a window, he heard a shot ring out and then a blood-curdling scream. Had they shot Julia?

Troy ran around to the back door, eased up and peaked through the window. He slowly turned the handle and let it swing open. He pulled the gun from the back of his pants, held it up, and moved through the kitchen, his eyes scanning every direction. Another shot and another scream. Definitely Julia. Outrage filled his body and he blasted forward without caution.

THIRTEEN

Troy moved through the foyer and up the stairs. The hallway was empty, so he walked slowly, keeping the noise to a minimum. With no lights on, the house was falling into darkness, making it difficult to see what might be lurking in dark corners. He held his gun ready, moving it with his line of sight. A door was cracked open and he could see movement inside. What were they doing to her?

He edged closer. A man in a police uniform was walking around. His form kept moving in and out of view through the small gap. The door swung open and Officer Green stepped into the hallway. As their eyes met, Green reached for his service pistol, but Troy pulled the trigger twice, in quick succession, putting the man down as he was drawing his gun.

Troy continued into the room, knowing

there was at least one more man in the house, possibly others. There weren't any sounds. Where was Julia? He hadn't heard any more screams or even a whimper. Was she dead? Pushing the door the rest of the way open with the tip of his gun, Troy quickly scanned the room. A home office that had been torn apart. The furniture was upended, papers strewn about, ceramics broken into pieces on the floor. No Julia.

Turning back to the hallway, he continued to the next room. The door was open and the room was dark. He eased in slowly. No one there. Only one bedroom left. She had to be in there. Dread mixed with angst in his gut, turning his stomach sour. What would he find when he opened that last door?

Marty's voice boomed through the walls. "Where is it? This is your last chance!"

Troy burst through the third door in a very uncharacteristically impulsive reaction. Marty was ready. Before Troy could get his bearings in the room, something swung hard into Troy's back, sending him toppling over, his gun fumbling from his grasp. As he hit the floor, he saw Julia huddled in the corner, holding her legs to her chest. Blood was dripping into the carpet on her right side. One of them had shot her. He jumped to his feet and charged into Marty, letting his anger fuel his tired body. The man was better equipped than Troy had expected, but still fell short in comparison to Troy's abilities. He had Marty subdued and unconscious in a matter of seconds.

He ran to Julia's side. "How bad is it? Where are you hit?" He scanned her body until he found the entry point on her right thigh.

"It's in the muscle. I'm fine. No major arteries." Her bottom lip and cheek were bleeding. Her left upper arm was bruised. They had really roughed her up. A thick knot formed in his throat. Fear mixed with rage. He wasn't used to such a strong combination of emotions. She could have died. The idea of them putting their hands on her tensed every muscle fiber in his body. He wanted to punish the men who had hurt her. But he knew Julia wouldn't want that. And he was sure God wouldn't either. He had to focus on taking care of Julia. The law would decide punishment for these evil men.

Julia's eyes shot up. Troy turned his head to follow her gaze. A gruff-looking man stood in the doorway holding a shotgun pointed right at them. A shot rang out and the man fell back into the hallway. Troy turned to see Julia drop his handgun to the floor.

"That was the man from the cabin." Her voice was low. Tired.

Troy jumped up to make sure the man wouldn't get back up and saw that she'd winged him. His right shoulder was bleeding and he couldn't move his arm. Troy pulled some twine from his pocket and walked over. Grabbing the man's right arm, he twisted it back, forcing him onto his stomach. The man screamed out in pain. Troy secured his wrists together and then his feet. He was about to step away then decided to tie the guy's feet to his hands with another piece of twine, ensuring he wouldn't be a threat. He quickly did the same to Marty Wilcox. Officer Green was too badly injured to be a threat.

Tory went back to Julia and carefully lifted her off the floor after tucking his gun into the back of his waistband. "Are there any more of them?" When Julia shook her head no, he carried her down the stairs and out the back door.

She lost consciousness before she could tell him anything more. He checked the area before walking out front. Then he placed her in the passenger seat of the Jeep, quickly securing her seat belt. Luckily, the keys were in the ignition. He drove down to where Jake was hiding and stopped. The sky had fallen into complete darkness. The clouds had come back while he had been inside. There weren't any stars or even a hint of the moon.

"Jake." Troy called out, hoping the boy hadn't left. A moment later, the bush rustled and Jake came running, carrying Troy's backpack over one shoulder. "Quick, get in." As soon as he jumped over the side, Troy drove off, not wanting to be around if anyone else showed up. He thought about calling Leo, but needed to tend to Julia's wound first. He drove a few blocks away and then pulled over.

Jake had been leaning forward, watching Julia, panic shrouding his features. A lone tear ran down his cheek. He quickly wiped it away and sniffled. "Will she be okay?"

"She'll be fine. Don't worry." Troy grabbed his backpack from Jake and pulled a knife and a small flashlight from a side pocket. He had Jake hold the light as he cut open the leg of Julia's pants to get a better look at the wound. He pulled his shirt off and tore it nearly in two, then he tied it around Julia's leg and knotted the fabric.

"We'll get her somewhere safe so I can clean her up." He sent a quick text to Leo, telling him to dispatch an ambulance and officers to Jake's house, then sped off.

A cool breeze sent a painful shiver through Julia's body. Her eyes were opening, but everything was hazy. It was so dark. She felt movement. Where was she? She tried pushing herself up, but pain ripped through her right leg, causing her to wince.

"We're almost there. Don't try to move." Troy turned to her with a reassuring glance. He was driving her through the woods again.

"Where's Jake?" Julia panicked. She had no idea if he had gotten away.

Jake leaned forward from behind her. "I'm here." He looked down at her leg. "Does it hurt bad?" His eyes lifted to meet hers, sadness making them heavy.

Julia wanted to cry for all this boy had seen. "It's not so bad." She'd lied, not wanting him to worry. It was agony like she had never experienced before. But she knew it would be fine as long as she could clean it out and have some time to heal. It was difficult to believe she would have that opportunity under the current circumstances.

"Where are we going?" Julia braced her hands on the sides of her seat, pushing herself up. She could see they were in the woods, but it was too dark to know if it was familiar.

"We have to go back to the cabin to get the drive. I hid it behind the paneling in the bedroom. I'll stitch you up there. Then we'll figure out where to go and lay low for a few days." He glanced over at her. "Sit back and rest. Only five more minutes."

Julia leaned back and closed her eyes, trying to ignore the pain that shot through her thigh with every bump and jostle. She clasped her hands together under her chin. *Lord, please help us. We have nearly died so many times. We need Your guidance. Your intervention, if it's Your will to do so. Please let Jake and Troy make it through this.*

Julia opened her eyes as Troy pulled the Jeep up against the cabin, where it had been when she and Jake had released the brake and let it roll down the hill that morning. It had been a mistake. She should have waited for Troy. So many bad things had happened because of that one decision. She would be more cautious going forward. And the three of them would stay together. No more splitting up. No more unilateral decisions. Julia realized that she was the one who'd broken that promise, not Troy.

Once inside, Troy pulled out his first-aid kit and laid it on the small counter. "How do you want to do this? We have to get the bullet out and close the wound."

Julia was lying on the small couch. "Do you have anything resembling tweezers in that kit?" When Troy nodded, she thought for a moment. "Help me over to the counter."

Troy picked her up and sat her on the small island, with her legs bent over the sides of the counter. She went through the kit, taking out what she needed. "Jake, I want you to go into the bedroom and stay there until we're done. You may hear me yell out. What I'm about to do is going to hurt, but I'll be fine. Stay in there until I tell you to come out."

Jake stared for a moment. He looked at the bleeding wound on her leg then met her eyes. "Do you promise?"

"Come over here." He walked over slowly. "Closer." She pulled him in and kissed his head. "I promise. I need to focus on what I have to do. I don't want you to worry about me."

Jake nodded and went into the bedroom. He closed the door quietly, watching her until he couldn't. Julia felt it would be better if he didn't see her in more pain. She would try to keep the noise to a minimum.

Troy had already begun sterilizing the things she would need. "I'll pull the bullet out. I can stitch it, too." He cut the leg of her pants off above the wound and let it drop to the floor.

Julia shook her head. "No, I'll do that. I think I can pull out the bullet myself."

Troy rolled up a small dish towel and held it out to her. "Bite down on this. I'm doing the bullet. You can guide me, but you can't do this yourself." Then he undid the tourniquet he must have tied around her leg when she'd passed out earlier.

Julia bit down on the towel and leaned back on her hands, tilting her head up. Better not to watch. There would be too much anticipation of pain. A moment later, she was biting down with force, trying to keep from screaming out. Tears streamed down her cheeks as she held back the cries edging up her throat. Sweat began to glide down her back. A sudden stinging had her jolting up to see that Troy was pouring peroxide into the wound.

He looked up at her. "The bullet's out. Are you sure you don't want me to stitch it up?"

Julia released the towel from between her teeth. "I'll do it. I imagine my way will leave less damage."

Troy nodded, smiling. "I don't doubt that. Let me know if you need me to step in." He handed her the threaded needle.

Julia splashed the peroxide all over her hands, letting it spill everywhere, then put the towel back in her mouth. She took in a deep breath through her nose, closed her eyes and blew it out slowly, then opened her eyes and got started. The first stroke of the needle was the hardest. After that, she was prepared for what it would feel like. Not that knowing minimized the excruciating pain.

When she was done, Troy was ready with a bandage that he'd already covered in ointment. He wrapped gauze around her leg to hold it in place. Then he stepped back, shaking his head.

"What?" Julia stared at him, wondering if there was something she'd missed.

"I can't believe you just did that." He stared down at her leg. "I heard a second shot. Are you hit anywhere else? I couldn't find anything."

"Marty shot at the wall next to my head to scare me. That was when I scurried into the corner." Julia realized Troy wasn't wearing a shirt. He was even more muscular than she had thought. It wasn't hard to believe what he was capable of, seeing how he was built. The man was perfectly sculpted.

Troy's eyebrows pinched together as he stepped closer. He picked her up and carried her to the couch. "We can't stay here. I'll finish cleaning you up, grab the drive, and we'll go."

He poured peroxide on a thick piece of gauze and wiped her bottom lip and left cheek.

After how painful taking care of her leg had been, the little bit of stinging on her lip and face didn't feel so bad. Julia realized that she had never felt taken care of in this way. Her mother had done what was required, but Julia had never felt this safe. This sense of concern for her well-being. There was always something more important than spending time with Julia. Her parents kept a busy social calendar and they'd never allowed her to get in the way of that. Not even when she was sick. Looking up at this man, who was taking such great care to make sure she was all right, Julia felt a surge of warmth radiating through her chest.

When Troy was done, he stared down at her with a mix of emotion in his eyes. Julia wasn't sure what he was thinking. She saw some anger—not much of a surprise given all that had happened—but there was something else. As much as she wanted to know, it didn't seem like the right time to ask. Jake was waiting in the bedroom.

"We should tell Jake he can come out." Without another word, the bedroom door opened and Jake joined them. "I guess you were listening?" Julia couldn't help but smile at him. She was aware of how much Jake had come to care for her, too. It made her long for the kind of family she had given up on a long time ago.

Spending time with Troy and Jake gave her a renewed hope. There were people out there who would treat her with kindness. Julia knew that Jake would eventually go back to his mother and Troy would return to his own life. She would miss them, but she was so grateful to have been able to know them. Even if it would only be for a short time. Even if Troy had been the first man to reach a place in her heart that had been closed off for as long as she could remember.

Jake smiled and sat next to her. "You didn't scream at all."

"It wasn't so bad." Julia smiled at the boy, hoping to put him at ease. She noticed Troy's eyebrows go up and then he turned and went into the bedroom.

"I've got it. We should go." Troy came out, shoving the drive into the front pocket of his jeans. Then he pulled a navy blue T-shirt from his backpack and put it on. The combination of the dark shirt and his nearly black hair made his bright blue eyes practically glow. He was one of the most beautiful men she had ever seen.

She tried to think about where they could hide. "There's a B and B just outside of town. I deliver baked goods there. I can call the owner and arrange for us to go in through the back door so no one sees us. He's a nice man."

Troy shook his head. "Too many civilians that could get caught in the crossfire. Too many people who might let someone know where we are. I think I know where we should go. I should have thought of it sooner. Maybe we could have avoided some of this." He packed everything back into his bag and handed it to Jake. "Can you carry this for me, buddy?"

Jake took the pack and Troy walked over to pick up Julia. "I'll carry you out."

Julia lifted her arm. "Help me up. I want to try and walk."

"Tomorrow. Give it at least a day to start healing. We'll see what it looks like in the morning." Knowing he was right, she let him scoop her up and carry her outside. Jake opened the passenger door then jumped into the back seat. As Troy placed Julia in the front, the whole area lit up. He quickly closed her door and turned toward the bright light. She was helpless to do anything useful. She watched him pull the gun from the back of his pants and point it at the bright headlights that were approaching fast. There was no way out.

Julia tried to pull herself up, but dropped right down, the pain in her leg too intense to even consider trying to run. She signaled for Jake to get down. He curled into a ball on the floor behind the driver's seat. They shouldn't have stayed there to stitch her leg. They should've gotten the drive and left. Waiting another hour wouldn't have made a difference. It hadn't been long enough for infection to set in.

The car rolled to a stop about ten yards away. She almost called out to Troy when she saw him start walking toward the car with his gun raised. What good would it do? She knew it wouldn't stop him. Her heart pounded against her ribs, a flush of panic depleting what was left of her energy.

Troy stopped halfway between her and the car. "Get out and show me your hands." He stood as still as stone, his muscles stiff with tension.

The driver's door opened, but it was impossible to see anything with the headlights shining in her eyes. She heard the crunch from someone's feet stepping onto the dead leaves. A dark figure stood tall behind the door.

"Come out where I can see you." Troy's

voice was calm and commanding. "Tell me who you are and why you're here. You have about two seconds before I put two bullets in your chest." He took a step closer, the gun trained on the dark form standing behind the door.

Julia could see Troy's finger tightening on the trigger in the light from the car. The only question was: Who would shoot first?

FOURTEEN

Troy tensed his trigger finger. Even if he got shot, he could squeeze two off, giving Julia a chance to get away with Jake. He watched the dark figure move around the car door. His hands raised above his head as he stepped in front of the light.

"Don't shoot. I'm unarmed. This is my cabin. I come up to check on it when it's empty. I'm not here to hurt anyone. Would you please point that thing away from me?" The man stood very still.

Troy waved the gun at the cabin. "Step over here, so I can see you better." The man moved toward the front door. "Put your hands against the wall. Spread your feet apart." Once he did, Troy walked over and checked him for a weapon. Finding none, he put his gun back into his waistband and stepped away. The man turned to face him.

"This is really your cabin?" Troy watched for any change in the man's expression.

He nodded. "Yes, it is."

"I'm sorry to have reacted to you that way. We've been dealing with some trouble. I didn't mean to involve you. You should know, we stayed here last night. I'll be happy to reimburse you another time. Right now, we need to go."

The man looked over at Julia and Jake, who had popped his head up. He shook his head. "No need. I have a decent idea of what's going on here. I'd rather not get involved. If my cabin helped you out, I'm glad for that. But if you don't mind, keep that information to yourselves. And please leave me out of it." He stuffed his shaking hands into his front pockets.

Troy wondered what he knew. For a such a big guy, he looked terrified. As much as he wanted to ask questions, Troy knew the man wasn't going to give him any answers.

Troy extended his hand. "I appreciate your help. You have my word. I won't mention meeting you." The man put his hand out and shook, quickly pulling away.

Troy headed for the Jeep, continuing to watch the man. He drove off, into the darkness, relieved that it hadn't been another altercation.

The aftermath of what he had been forced to do was hollowing out his insides. When he'd seen Julia's condition, something had snapped inside, challenging his self-control. This unwelcome rush of feelings had him off balance. He was pretty sure he might be falling in love with her, which seemed ridiculous given the short time they'd known each other. Every time he looked at her, there was something that grew warmer in his chest. It made him feel a little less broken with each day.

Then there was Jake. The boy's innocence had been stolen and Troy was having a very difficult time reconciling that fact. He had grown to care deeply for the boy and resented that his childhood had been sullied with the darkness that had invaded Bluerock. If this had been a mission with the SEALs, things would have been handled by now. And it wouldn't have boded well for those with dishonorable intentions. But he wasn't a soldier anymore and there were no orders to follow. There were different rules in normal society. The conflict of his need to protect and his need to live by a code of ethics warred inside him.

He felt Julia's hand on his, bringing him out of the churning turmoil that didn't seem to have an answer. He wove his fingers through hers, letting her touch ground him.

"I know of a place they shouldn't be able to connect to us." Troy's phone rang from his pocket. He had to let go of Julia's hand to see who was calling. "It's the chief."

Troy put it on speaker. "Hey, Leo."

"What happened in that house? Who shot my officer?" Leo's voice thundered with anger.

"I did. He's with them. It was him or me. I'm sorry, Leo." He listened to the long silence. "I'm taking them out of town for a while. I need you to figure out what's going on here so Jake can see his mother and Julia can get back to her own life."

Leo huffed with frustration then his tone softened. "Green really tried to shoot you?"

"He was pulling his gun, so, yeah I'm pretty sure he intended to use it." Troy could hear his friend's disappointment.

"I'm sorry. That's on me. These guys are my responsibility. Where will you go?"

"I'm not sure yet. I'll figure something out. We're already a good distance away." Troy noticed Julia's eyes widen on him. She had to be wondering why he was lying to his friend. "I'll be in touch in a few days. Hopefully, you'll have good news by then."

"Be careful. I'll call when I have something."

"Sounds good." Troy disconnected and turned off his phone. Then he popped it open and removed the battery.

Julia was still eyeing him with uncertainty. "Why did you tell him we were already out of town? What if someone sees us and tells him?"

"We know at least two cops were involved. We have no idea how many more could be dirty. I know Leo means well, but he clearly has no idea who to trust. I can't take any more risks. Too much has happened to both of you already." He took her hand in his and laced their fingers together. "I almost lost you." He lifted the back of her hand to his lips, placing a light kiss there, then returned their clasped hands to the console between them.

It wasn't lost on Troy that Julia may not be feeling the same way. He didn't doubt that she cared for him, but that didn't mean she saw any kind of future for them. She would probably want to get as far as possible from him and this town when it was all over. She had been through so much. He could admit that she seemed to be handling it well, but that was no indication of her desire to stay. He wanted to ask, but didn't want to make things awkward if she wasn't feeling any of what he was.

He hadn't been lying about getting them out of town. Troy made his way through the woods, keeping off the roads. The lake house was technically in the next town, but so close to the border, it might as well have been in Bluerock. The terrain made for a bumpy ride, which wasn't ideal for Julia, but there was too much of a risk of being seen again on the roads. By the time they arrived, an hour and a half later, Julia had fallen asleep and Jake was looking pretty drowsy. Troy got out and punched in the code for the garage door so he could pull inside. He just hoped no one would connect him with this place.

The sun filled the room with morning light, easing Julia from slumber. She had a vague recollection of arriving last night, but had been so tired, she'd barely opened her eyes when Troy had carried her in. Her bed was big and cozy, with plush blankets and pillows. The windows stretched from the floor to the high ceiling and spanned across an entire wall. There were a few paintings on the walls that looked as if they could have been done locally. She wondered where she was and what the rest of the place looked like.

She sat up and carefully swung her legs over the side of the bed. She could see endless tall trees through the windows. It was so peaceful. She edged off the side, keeping her weight on her good leg. Walking wasn't going to be easy, but she wanted to see more of this beautiful house. And she wanted to check on Jake. Leaning on furniture and walls, Julia hobbled her way out of the room. The door opened into a vast living space with windows that reached an even higher ceiling with views of a lake in the distance.

There was a delicious aroma permeating the house, making her mouth water. Troy was on the other side of the living room, in an open kitchen with light wood cabinets and creamy stone countertops. The couches were made of a worn brown leather with a dark wood coffee table between them. There was more artwork on the walls that weren't made of glass, and what looked like family photographs placed on a few shelves in a wall unit. Everything about this space felt warm and welcoming, with a strong sense of home.

Troy looked up and immediately came over to her. "Wait right there. I'll help you. How are you feeling this morning? You slept for nearly ten hours."

"I feel rested for the first time in a long time. That bed is incredible." Troy put his arm around her back. "This place is beautiful. Do you know the owner?"

Troy helped her over to a soft leather seat at the kitchen table. "You might say that. I'm cooking eggs and toast. The bread was frozen, but it's decent. I got the eggs out of the neighbor's chicken coop about a half mile away. Another person I owe when this is over. Are you hungry?"

"Famished. Where's Jake?" She looked around, wondering if he was up yet.

"He's in his room. He ate already. I think he's taking a shower. There are plenty of clothes here. Take whatever you want. There's a bathroom in your bedroom. I'll help you get set up after you eat something."

"Troy, who does this house belong to?" Her eyes drifted over the exposed wood beams on the ceiling. Every inch of this place was perfect.

"Oh, right." He dished out her breakfast and put it down in front of her. "It's mine. I don't come here much. It seemed like a good place to hide. No one knows about it. Unless they start searching public records, but I don't see why they would."

Julia's eyes widened. "This is yours? Why don't you live here full-time? Not that your house in town isn't nice, but this place feels more like a home."

"I don't really have the answer to that. I bought it about a month after moving to Bluerock. I put everything that mattered to me in this house. But I haven't been able to bring myself to move in."

Julia knew he was probably punishing himself in some way. She wanted to ask, but sensed that Troy might not be ready to talk about that yet. She pointed to the pictures in the wall unit across the room. "Are you in those photos?"

He followed her line of sight. "Yes." He went and took one off the shelf.

Julia started eating, unable to resist fresh, hot food. "This is really good."

He handed her the picture. "Not as good as your cooking, but it'll do. This is me with my mother and my sister, right before we lost our mom." His voice trailed off a little.

"You guys look so happy. Your mom and sister are beautiful. They look so much like you." They had the same dark hair and stunning blue eyes.

Troy took the seat next to hers. "Thank you. My sister will love hearing that you think we look alike. She always tells me we could pass for twins and I always tell her she's crazy." He laughed a little. "My mom would have liked you. You remind me of her."

"That's a very sweet thing to say." Julia was warmed by such a kind sentiment. Troy had been opening up and becoming warmer with her, but last night he'd told Leo that she needed to get back to her own life. Was he looking forward to being rid of her? It didn't matter. She would enjoy her time with him while she could.

Jake came out and ran over to her. "Does

your leg hurt?" He was wearing fresh sweat-pants, which had been cut to the length of his legs, and a sweatshirt that had been adjusted to fit his arms in the same way.

"It does, but not like last night. All I need is a little time to heal. How did you sleep?"

"Fine. I'm still kind of hungry. Are there more eggs?" Jake looked at Troy.

"There are, but I have other things if you want to look at your options. Check in the pantry. I keep crackers and cookies in there. Lots of different cans of soup. Pasta and sauce. Take whatever you want." Troy got up and put the picture back on the shelf. "There's ice cream in the freezer. Hopefully, it isn't freezer burned."

Julia finished her breakfast. "I don't see a shower happening, but I should get cleaned up. I'm guessing I'll be wearing more of your sister's clothes?" He nodded. "Are you sure she won't mind? I've already ruined an outfit."

"I can assure you she doesn't care. The clothes are from her last closet overhaul, as she calls it. She was getting rid of it all. I suggested she keep some things here, for when she comes to visit. I never anticipated a situation like this." He helped her up.

Jake came out of the pantry with a box of chocolate-chip cookies and a wide smile. "Does the TV work?" How was it possible that he still had so much childlike innocence?

"It should. The remote is in that drawer." Troy pointed to an end table next to the couch.

He helped Julia hobble back to her room. "I called the hospital this morning and spoke to his mother. She's doing better, but she'll be in there for a while. She's probably safer that way."

"Did you tell Jake?" Julia sat on the bed while Troy gathered clothes and towels from one of the two closets.

"He spoke to her. I think that's why he's in such good spirits. It's good for him to have her reassurance that she's getting better. I can help, if you want to wash your hair."

Julia stood on her good leg and let him assist her into the bathroom. She sat in the tub, still wearing the clothes she'd worn yesterday, and leaned her head back so Troy could wash her hair. Then he gave her privacy to undress and clean herself up. A thick bath towel was on the edge of the tub. She used it to dry off and soak up any remaining water in the tub so she could get dressed. It seemed to take forever. Once she finally managed to get the fresh clothes on, she called Troy back in to help her.

The three of them spent the day inside, not wanting to risk being seen wandering around by hikers. Troy said it was rare, but that people occasionally came through his property. It almost felt normal being there. As if there weren't people hunting them down with every intention of killing them.

Troy pulled out a deck of cards in the late afternoon, while the meat he'd defrosted was cooking, and taught Jake the games he'd played with his mother as a child. He would make a good father, if he ever wanted that for himself. Julia couldn't be sure. Troy had been living a pretty solitary life, from what she could see.

Troy had been right when he'd said talking to his mother had lifted Jake's spirits. The boy was laughing and enjoying beating Troy at cards. He especially liked having a heaping bowl of ice cream after dinner. Julia smiled more that day than she had in years. Watching them having fun together brought her so much joy. She thanked God for this time to heal in a safe place. She prayed that Troy's friend, Leo, would finally accept what was happening and find a quick resolution.

Troy kept the lights off as the sky grew dark, instead burning logs in the stone fireplace. The soft glow gave the house a different warmth than what she'd seen in the daylight. It somehow revealed a softer side of the man, as well.

When it was time for Jake to go to bed, he came over and threw his arms around her. "Good night, Julia." He kissed her cheek and followed Troy into the bedroom.

After tucking him in, Troy returned and sat next to her. "It's good to see him that way. I was worried how this situation would affect him." He shifted closer and lightly ran his fingers over her face and lips. "Does this hurt? It looks a lot better today."

She leaned into his touch. "I don't really notice it much." Julia looked into his blue eyes. He was staring at her again. He had done this before, but never so close. She wondered what it meant. What he might be thinking. There was so much intensity behind that gaze.

"I'm glad." He dropped his hand, leaving her missing the feel of his touch.

Julia watched the way the light of the fire danced across his masculine features. "How about you? You were in a car accident and you've been in a few fights. How are you feeling?" They had both been attacked so many times. She was so grateful Jake hadn't been harmed since she'd met him. She knew he had been grabbed that first night, but no one had physically hurt him since. Marty Wilcox certainly hurt him in a different way.

"I'm fine. I've been through much worse." Troy glanced down at her leg. "It was hard for me not to hurt Marty for that." He stared at the fresh bandage he had helped her with earlier that evening. "My training made me dangerous to people like him. But I know I can't allow that to consume me." He looked into her eyes. "And I didn't want to scare you again."

Julia dropped her eyes. She had forgotten how fearful she had been the first time she'd seen Troy. It was different now. "I know I'm safe with you. But I'm glad you didn't allow them to pull you down. You're better than that. I told you, the Lord has a plan for you. You've already showed what kind of a man you are. Be patient. He'll reveal Himself to you."

"I've thought about that a lot. I hope you're right."

Julia looked him directly in the eye. "I think I am. Give it time." She felt her face flush when Troy leaned closer. The intensity of his stare was a little intimidating. Her eyes dropped. "What are you thinking right now?"

He curled his finger under her chin and gently lifted until her eyes met his. "I'm wondering how you would feel if I kissed you."

Julia's heart raced in her chest. Her lips parted at the thought of what that would be like. Butterflies fluttered deep in her belly. She didn't move when he leaned nearer. She would tell him she wanted him to kiss her, but she couldn't form any words. He moved a little more, his lips hovering just above hers. She tried to force herself to breathe as she tilted her head up. His mouth was soft and gentle. He slid his fingers along the sides of her face, into her hair, and deepened the kiss. She had never experienced anything like it. Warmth filled her body, making her feel a connection to him she hadn't ever had with anyone.

When Troy leaned back, Julia opened her eyes and couldn't help but stare at the full lips that had just been on hers. They looked different to her now. Before, they'd seemed stern and sometimes harsh. Now, she had a better sense of the gentle heart he had been guarding. She hoped he felt as safe with her as she did with him. And that he might feel at least some of the affection she could no longer deny.

"We should get some sleep." He stood and pulled her to her feet. She hobbled along, allowing herself to lean on him.

Once he helped her into bed and pulled the blankets up over her body, she finally found the ability to speak. "Thank you for everything, Troy. You've done so much for us."

He kissed her forehead and hovered close. "You don't ever need to thank me. You've done as much for me, if not more." He kissed each corner of her mouth then pressed his lips to hers one more time before stepping back. "Sleep well, Julia." Then he was gone.

Staring at the shadows the tall trees cast on the ceiling in the moonlight, Julia pressed her fingers to her lips, still feeling the sensation of his kiss. What did it mean? So much had changed between them. Her eyes began to feel heavy and she allowed herself to drift off, thinking about the sweet man who had cracked open her defenses and made her feel the kind of warmth she had only ever imagined.

Then her body jolted upright. Where was the drive? There had to be a computer in this house, given all of the other modern conveniences she'd noticed. Troy had to have checked the contents by now. Why hadn't he mentioned it?

FIFTEEN

Yesterday had been a good day. One of the best Troy could remember. He stretched out in his bed as he realized he had slept past sunrise for the first time in years. He glanced over at the alarm panel, noting that nothing was amiss. Each zone was solid red, meaning everything was still armed. He smiled as he stood up, thinking of that kiss last night. Maybe he and Julia could spend more time getting to know each other when this was over. He was feeling more optimistic about what his future might look like. Maybe he wouldn't spend his life alone. Maybe he could have more.

He walked out into the living room, considering what to make for breakfast. He imagined his guests wouldn't be up for at least another hour. He headed for the kitchen, then froze. He turned to see Julia sitting on the couch. She was so still.

His hand flattened on his chest. "You startled me. What are you doing up so early?"

"Where's the drive?" Julia's tone was so cold.

"What? In my safe." He walked over and stood in front of her.

"Did you look at it yet?" Her expression was like stone, nothing resembling the gentle kindness he had grown used to seeing.

"Yes. What's wrong?"

"When did you look at it, exactly?" She tilted her head slightly.

"Two nights ago, when we first got here. Why? What's going on with you?"

"Why didn't you tell me?"

"Things were so nice here yesterday. I thought everyone could use one good day, without having to think about all of the horrible things that've been happening. You don't need to worry about it. I'm handling it." Troy didn't understand why Julia seemed so angry.

"What does that mean? How are you handling it?" Her eyebrows pulled together.

"Look, I don't think you need to worry about this. I have a very specialized skill set and I made a lot of connections during my time as a SEAL. It's better if I handle this end of things."

Julia rose, using the arm of the couch, keeping her voice low, but there was definitely a lot of anger there. "We agreed, no more unilateral decisions. Why didn't you show me? Or tell me what was on it? Or discuss whatever it is you've decided to do without my knowledge?"

Troy put his hands up, feeling a little defensive. "Are you kidding me right now? You want to talk about unilateral decisions? What about the one you made to leave the cabin that kicked off a whole string of events that never had to happen?" He regretted his words immediately, knowing Julia felt responsible for his car accident.

Her eyes widened. "So, you do blame me?"

"No, of course not. You couldn't have known what would happen. I'm saying that you should trust me by now. How long have you been sitting here waiting to confront me?"

She stared at him for a moment. "What did you do with the drive?"

"I told you, it's in my safe." He took a step

back, growing increasingly frustrated. This was his arena. Not hers. Why would she question him? Why didn't she realize that he knew what he was doing? Hadn't he proven himself already? "There are some things it would be best not to share with you. It's for your own safety."

Her eyebrows shot up, along with the pitch of her voice. "At what point have I been safe through any of this? Nothing you tell me will make a difference… Are you protecting your friend?"

"Stop! It's my fault! All of it! Don't argue!" Jake ran into the room, his face bright red and his body so stiff with tension that Troy became immediately concerned.

"Nothing is your fault, buddy. Come sit down. We can talk about it." Troy gestured to the couch as Julia held her arms open to him. "You need to calm down."

"*No!* You don't understand! Everything that happened is my fault. To you guys. My parents. All of it. Everything is because of me!" He ran to the front door, fumbled with the locks, pulled it open and ran outside.

Troy had to disarm the alarm before chasing Jake or the blaring siren would start echoing through the entire forest in less than a minute. He turned to tell Julia he'd go and get Jake when he realized she was already outside, hobbling toward the lake, using an umbrella as a makeshift cane. She was getting around better than yesterday. She'd been lucky that Marty had carried a .22-caliber handgun. It hadn't done nearly as much damage as the guns the other men carried would have.

He rushed to her side. "Let me help you."

"Go ahead. He needs one of us now. He needs to know he isn't to blame for anything. I'll make my way there. Go help him." Julia was insistent, so Troy ran for the lake.

Jake was pacing back and forth along the small dock. Troy had no idea if the boy knew how to swim. He ran faster, getting to Jake in a few seconds. Then he had no idea what to say. He had no experience with children.

"Please move away from the edge. It's very deep at this end." Troy held his hand out. "Let's go talk to Julia. I know she's very worried about you."

Jake's sad little eyes lifted, filled with tears that would tip over the edge at any moment.

He walked away from the edge. "You should help her." Jake nodded at Julia.

"She told me to talk to you. The thing is, I'm not really sure what to say. I do know one thing. None of this is your fault."

He shook his head. "You don't understand. When I tell you, you'll know. You'll both hate me because you'll know what I did."

"We could never hate you, Jake. That isn't possible." Julia's voice was filled with kindness. Troy turned to see her approaching. He held out a hand to help her step onto the dock. She immediately pulled Jake into her arms and let him cry. She didn't talk or ask any questions. She just let him get it all out.

After a few minutes, Jake stepped back, wiping his face with the sleeve of his sweatshirt. "I heard my dad talking to my mom. He was scared. He saw something bad in the old warehouse. He worked there at night sometimes, as a security guard. He told my mom that he took a video with his phone. The men there were doing something with drugs. He saw them. He said he called someone. I don't remember the letters."

Troy presumed Jake must be referring to the DEA, but couldn't be certain.

Julia put her hand on his shoulder. "Take your time. We're not going anywhere."

He nodded. "My dad loaded the video on his computer at home and made backups. My mother had one and Uncle Marty…" His voice trailed off. "But his was in an envelope my dad mailed. Uncle Marty probably didn't know he had it at first."

"None of this is your fault." Troy's stomach wrenched. These men had to be stopped.

Jake shook his head. "It is my fault. My dad's friend came over a few days later. He came up to my room to see why I wasn't out back for the barbecue. He could tell something was bothering me and he asked me to tell him. He was a cop, like my dad, so I told him what I'd heard. He said it was good that I told him. That he would help my dad. He put his arm around me and told me that I was becoming a man." His eyes cast down. "He came back in the middle of the night with some of the other cops. They kept hitting my dad. When he wouldn't tell them where the drive was, they hit my mom." He started crying. Julia pulled him in, but he pushed away.

"My dad said he would show them and my mom snuck out while he pulled it up on his computer. I was in the hallway, listening to everything. I froze. I should have called for help. I didn't know what to do." He was talking faster. "My mom took me with her downstairs. One of them grabbed me and she hit him over the head with a pan." Jake's fingers felt around the bruise on his upper arm.

"She got the drive out of the vase with the fake flowers and we ran outside. Then my dad's friend came out and shot her before we got out of the yard. She gave me the drive and told me to run. She said not to stop until I found a safe place." He looked up at Julia. "Then you got shot because I came to you." He broke down again.

Julia wrapped her arms around him and they both sank down onto the wood planks of the dock. Troy grabbed her from behind to keep them from falling. She looked up at him with tears in her eyes. Troy felt like he might explode. He knelt beside them and rubbed Jake's back.

"I understand why you feel like this is your fault, but it's not. Nothing you did was wrong. You confided in someone you should have been able to trust. Everything that happened after that is on him. He betrayed you and your family. You are not to blame. Do you hear what I'm saying? This isn't on you. It's on them." Troy stopped. He could feel the anger edging out. He didn't want to let Jake feel any of it.

"Troy's right. I could never blame you. All you've done is try to help." Julia was so gentle. So loving. Like his mother had been with him and his sister when they were children.

Jake lifted his head from Julia's shoulder. "You're not mad at me?"

"Never. Not even a little bit. You're the best kid I know." Julia held his hand in hers. "I've seen what those men do. That's their choice and they'll have to answer for it one day."

Jake looked at Troy. He shook his head. "No way. You're the bravest kid I've ever met. Telling an adult you trusted was exactly what you were supposed to do. He took advantage of you." Troy stood up. "We should get back inside. We can talk more in the house." He scanned the area, making sure no one was around.

"I'd like to sit by the water for a little while, if that's ok?" Jake looked up at Troy.

"I'll stay with him. He'll help me back to the house in five minutes." She turned to

Jake. "Right?" Her reassuring smile lightened the tension in Jake's expression.

"I'll help her, Troy. You can count on me this time." His words fell into Troy's stomach like a lead ball.

"I know I can count on you, Jake. I've never doubted it. Five minutes." Troy took another look around and started walking back to the house. He realized Jake might want to talk to Julia alone. She had a way of making it easier to let things out. He didn't want to interfere with that. It was only the beginning of what Jake would need to get through this.

He waited at the window, watching for any movement. They sat with their legs hanging over the side of the dock, Julia's arm around Jake's shoulders. Something shifted in the trees. He leaned forward to look closer. It had to be an animal. No one would know to find them here. Troy exhaled with relief when a young fawn trotted out, followed by the mother.

Standing there, waiting impatiently, he tried to come up with a way to smooth things over with Julia. It hadn't been fair to turn the tables on her. He had promised not to make big decisions without her and he knew that she believed leaving him behind had been for his benefit. He wasn't used to having to answer to anyone. He'd led most of the missions he'd participated in, with the exception of his first year. And he hadn't ever had to work with anyone lacking the training he'd had. This was very messy. There were feelings and fears he had to consider, making everything so much more complicated.

A man walked out of the trees. He was dressed for a hike, so Troy wasn't sure he was a threat. Troy pressed a hidden latch in the side of the wall unit, releasing the shelf. He swung it open and grabbed his pistol. Another man appeared and they both pulled guns out as they walked toward Julia and Jake, who were completely unaware of what was coming.

Julia heard two popping sounds and turned to see what it was. A man dropped to the ground about thirty yards away. Troy was standing halfway between the house and the tree line, his gun raised. Then he took another two shots. Julia shifted her gaze and saw another man drop. How had they been found? She tried to stand, forced to lean on Jake for support. They had to get back to the house.

She looked up and saw Troy running to them. A man appeared on the dock, pointing a gun at Jake. She felt him stiffen beside her as she tried to shift in front of him.

"Please don't. He's just a child." She tried pleading, because there was little else she could do in her current condition. The man smiled with a kind of darkness she had never come face to face with before.

A moment later, Troy tackled the gunman, dragging him into the lake. Julia stood on the edge, trying to see, but the water was too dark. Jake grabbed her hand, squeezing so tight her fingers ached.

At first a lot of bubbles came to the surface, but then there was nothing. The water was almost still. Julia began to panic. What was happening down there? Would Troy survive? What would she do if he didn't? She had been so angry with him. Now all she could do was beg God to let him be all right. She needed him to be all right. None of what had happened earlier mattered. He had become so important to her.

The water shifted wildly and Julia realized it might not be Troy coming to the surface. She looked around for anything she could use to stop that man from getting out and hurting Jake. Her pulse raced, making her head spin.

"Get away from the water." She pushed Jake toward the grass. "Go to the house and lock the door. I'll be right behind you." He stared at her, shaking his head. She knew he wouldn't want to leave her behind, but she couldn't protect him. "Go! Run! Now!" Once he left, she turned back to the water, leaning her weight on her good leg.

A rush of movement brought a head to the surface, and then another. Troy reached up and pulled himself onto the dock, then he turned and yanked the other man out. His hands and feet were bound behind his back with twine. The man coughed out water and tried desperately to catch his breath. She turned and saw Troy standing upright, barely fazed by the exertion. His blue eyes met hers and she couldn't feel anything but gratitude.

Without thinking, Julia threw her arms around him. "Thank you, God," she whispered. Then she felt Troy's strong, wet arms envelope her. She didn't care if he soaked her. All that mattered was that he was alive. She looked up and saw Jake running their way.

Troy pulled him in and Julia rested her

head on Troy's wet shirt. Everything had happened so fast. She hadn't had a moment to consider what this meant. They weren't safe *anywhere*. How long had those men been waiting for them to come outside? It began to feel as though their luck was running out. Eventually, a time would come when Troy wouldn't be able to get to them before it was too late. It seemed inevitable. She looked down at Jake and began to cry. *Please let us make it through, Lord. Guide us to an end to this madness.*

SIXTEEN

Troy knew what had to be done now. There was no getting out of town. These guys were organized and seemed to have eyes everywhere. He remembered how shaken that man at the cabin had been. And Henry had seemed to have an awareness he wasn't willing to elaborate on. How had Troy missed something so malignant for an entire year? This town was corrupt and the people living there knew it. Why didn't he? Was it possible that Leo didn't know? How could he not? He had been the chief of the Bluerock police force for at least two years. He had been an officer before that.

After locking the house down and setting the alarm, Troy helped Julia into her room and gave her fresh clothes to wear. He did the same for Jake. Then he went into his own room and changed. He opened his safe and took out the drive. Now that this house had been compromised, he couldn't leave it behind. They wouldn't take the Jeep this time. He had an enclosed Polaris Ranger with a covered bed that he had filled with supplies the first night they'd arrived. There was plenty of nonperishable food—including MREs—weapons and ammunition, a few changes of clothes for each of them, water, sleeping bags and some other things he thought might be useful. The camouflage exterior would help it blend into the forest once they reached their destination.

He had to stop thinking like a civilian and use the skills he'd gained as a SEAL. He was beginning to see Julia's point about his training being for something important. He would keep them safe. Seeing Julia cry, knowing she was losing hope, only made him more determined. He had no intention of failing. He never had before. And he had been up against far more dangerous enemies. Allowing his emotions to cloud his thinking had been a mistake. It had put Julia and Jake at risk. It was because he cared so deeply for both of them that he was going to let his training guide him going forward.

Once he got Julia and Jake into the Ranger and parked it outside, he put the battery back into his cell phone and made a call. He locked up the house while he made sure his plan was firmly in place. Once that was done, he called Leo, who answered on the first ring.

"Where are you? I've been trying to reach you." Leo sounded on edge.

"I'm at the lake house. Three guys showed up here trying to kill us. I put two down and hogtied the other. Feel free to send paramedics." Troy wasn't sure he could trust his friend anymore and couldn't help the coldness in his tone.

"What lake house?" Was it possible that Leo really didn't know?

"Check public records. I have to go." Troy was about to disconnect when he heard Leo call his name.

"Troy, wait. Who came at you? Were they cops? I can't believe this is happening. I feel like my town isn't the place I thought it was."

"I don't know. They were dressed for a hike." Troy had never seen them before.

"Let me get you into some kind of witness protection. It's obviously not safe for you three to keep running around on your own.

Let me help." Troy felt a trickle of guilt for doubting him when he heard Leo's concern.

"No way. You don't even know who you can trust. You get things handled there. Until then, I'm going to put down anyone who comes near them." He waited, but Leo was uncharacteristically quiet. Troy didn't have time to ask why. He needed the police chief to do his job. "I'm done being gentle. It's time to dismantle them. Are you with me?"

He waited. He could hear Leo shifting in his squeaky desk chair. "I'm always with you. Don't ever doubt it. How do you want to play this?"

Troy felt a small bit of relief. "I'm going to make sure I have the high ground. The rest is up to you, Leo. Are you going to do your job? Or are you going to keep letting these guys run wild because you don't want to take down your friends?"

"You know I'll get the job done. How will I reach you?" Leo's resolute tone was exactly what Troy had been hoping to hear.

"I'll bring the walkie. The usual frequency."

"I'll be in touch."

Troy took the battery out of his phone and drove into the trees. The ride was quiet, but at least the Ranger was better equipped to handle the terrain. They had what they needed to hunker down for at least a week. Creature comforts weren't a priority. He hoped the people in his care would be able to handle what was coming next.

Julia sat quietly as Troy drove them through the woods. His demeanor had shifted considerably. All of the softness she had seen come to the surface was gone. He was stoic. There was no expression in his eyes. It was as if Troy had somehow flipped a switch and shut down that part of himself. She had never been able to do that. Was it a blessing or a curse to have that skill? Maybe a little of both, she conceded to herself.

He hadn't given any indication of where he was taking them. He'd barely spoken a word when he'd packed them into this vehicle, which had already been filled with supplies. When he had done that, she had no idea. He wasn't the most forthcoming and his current state didn't make her feel comfortable asking questions. Mostly, she was grateful that Troy always seemed to have a plan. Another move to make. And that maybe God had a hand in it.

The vehicle rolled to a stop up near Rocky Ridge. She had never been this close to it before. Huge rocks were bunched together all along the rim of the valley. It was incredible up close. Some were flat; others formed unusual shapes. She looked up and saw something resembling a tree fort, but far more elaborate than anything she had ever seen. Steel beams formed the bottom structure, with thick wood planks creating a floor and partial walls around the entire base, which was shaped like an octagon. There was a ladder made of thick cable that hung down along the trunk of the tree and led up through a hole to one side of the center. A thatched roof sat six to eight feet above the floor. Had Troy made this? Did anyone else know it was up here?

Jake's eyes brightened at the sight of it. What boy wouldn't love a tree house like this? "Are we going up there?" He pointed, unable to hide his fascination.

"Yes. We'll be staying up there until this is over. It may take a few days, but we have what we need. Once I have you both up there, I'll get the supplies out and hide the Ranger." He turned to Julia. "Let Jake head up, then I'll help you."

She nodded, unsure how to be around this version of Troy. He was almost robotic in the way he spoke. As if he didn't know her.

Jake moved up the ladder with ease. Then Troy lifted her off her feet, without warning, and brought her over to the tree.

"I can carry you over my shoulder or you can get on my back, but you'd have to be sure you could hold on." He looked down at her, tucked against his broad chest.

"I can climb myself." She searched his eyes but couldn't find any sign of the man who had so gently kissed her and tucked her into bed last night.

Troy set her down and waited. She began the climb and he was right behind her. His foot was always two rungs down and his body was directly behind hers. He moved when she moved. It seemed a little odd at first, but it did make her feel safer as she ascended higher. Heights had never been something she handled well. Knowing Troy was there to keep her from falling definitely made it easier to stomach the climb. It had to be at least thirty feet to the base of the fort. And her injured thigh wasn't making it any easier.

Once she reached the top, Troy pushed her

through the opening. "Stay up here. Don't close the hatch. I'm going to bring up supplies." Then he squeezed the ladder together and slid down in a matter of seconds.

Julia and Jake stepped away from the opening. Troy was moving quickly, dropping bags on the deck and sliding back down. After a few trips, he moved the Ranger out of sight then joined them in the tree fort. He pulled the ladder up, dropped the hatch closed and secured it. He moved with such efficiency. She watched him hang a pair of binoculars from a hook inside the outer wall. He set up three chairs he unfolded out of canvas sacks. Three sleeping bags were then rolled out on one side. The food and water were tucked into a corner. He put a backpack against the tree trunk and then looked around to see that everything was in its place.

Jake looked at Julia with a questioning glance and then turned to Troy. "What are we going to do up here?"

"Wait. If anyone comes, I'll handle it. I have some things in motion. This will be over pretty quickly." Troy knelt down on one knee in front of Jake. "How are you doing?"

Jake shrugged his shoulders. "I'm okay. Are we gonna sleep up here tonight?"

Troy smiled. "We are. I'll be right here if you need anything. Don't be scared. We have the high ground."

"The high ground?" Jake's forehead creased.

"No one can get to us up here. And we can see them coming from a good distance away. It gives us the advantage." Troy stood and picked up the binoculars. "I can see anything that moves for a mile with these. I'll be checking regularly."

"Can I see?" Jake looked at Troy expectantly.

Troy handed them over. "Be careful. This is the only pair I have." He pointed to something on the side. "Don't flip this switch. We'll do that when it gets dark. We'll be able to see things at night."

Jake's eyebrows shot up in surprise. "Cool." He put them to his eyes and turned in a big circle. "You can see far." Then he handed the binoculars back to Troy. "Will you let me see tonight, too?"

"Of course." Troy did his own scan, turning in all directions.

"What else do you have in there?" Jake pointed to the backpack.

Troy smiled. At least he wasn't being cold

with Jake. "I might have a few things you can check out. Let me see." He unzipped another compartment and took out a compass and a few other small gadgets. Jake's eyes widened. Troy put each item into a smaller bag he'd pulled out and then handed it to Jake.

"Be careful. Don't let anything fall. We may need some of these things."

"I won't." Jake sat on one of the sleeping bags, on the other side of the tree, and began experimenting with what Troy had given him.

Julia had taken one of the chairs and was looking out over the ridge. It was unlike anything she had ever seen. The valley went on endlessly and the sky was clear blue for as far as she could see. Shifting her gaze, this vantage point made the forest feel more majestic than menacing. She could see God's hands in everything around her. The way it all fit so perfectly together. It was breathtaking.

Troy took the seat next to hers. "How are you doing with our new accommodations?" She could see him watching her from the side.

"I trust that you know what you're doing. You seem to have thought of everything. And I can't complain about the view." She turned to see his eyebrows shoot up in surprise. "My only concern is the night. I imagine it gets pretty cold up here."

"My sleeping bags are made for freezing temperatures and I have sweatshirts made to keep us warm. They'll be big on you and Jake, but they'll keep you from freezing." He shifted in his chair. "So, you trust me now?" There was a hint of amusement in his tone.

"It's not that I don't trust *you*. I have a hard time with it in general. My parents made all of my decisions and I had very little say in my life, until I broke away from them." She really didn't want to get into this, but not explaining her reaction wouldn't be fair. And it would leave Troy believing it was something about him that gave her doubts.

"My parents often lied in order to get me to do what they wanted. I found myself in situations, forced to do things I hated, because of that deceit. Social functions, activities that were very different from what I was told. And it goes way beyond that. I felt very alone and unprotected. I never knew what would trigger the next admonishment. Either one of them could turn vicious without warning. And the dishonesty was constant.

"They lied to me, to each other, to their

friends. They were always plotting and manipulating. It took some time to realize that not everyone was like them after I left. You hit a nerve. I'm sorry. I haven't had to put my trust in anyone in a while." It had been a long time since she'd really thought about how things had been at home. The memories weighed on her and prevented her from sleeping at night, but she mostly avoided allowing herself to put any real focus on them.

It was too painful. Too difficult to admit that her mother had allowed her father to be so cruel. The woman had even taken part, in her own way. Her parents' lack of concern for her needs and their ability to cut her down created a sense of being lost in darkness as a child. Maybe the avoidance only kept those feelings lingering. Talking out loud to someone else felt a little like letting go. Maybe it was time to move forward and leave that part of her life behind.

Troy nodded. "I knew things were difficult with your parents, but I didn't realize it was like that. I understand having a hard time trusting. What I saw overseas left me a little cynical. Do you think you can give me the benefit of the doubt for a few more days?

After that, you're free to get as far from me as you want. For right now, please let me keep you safe."

His words knocked the wind out of her. Was this Troy's way of saying he didn't want to see her when this was over? She tried to smile. "Of course. I can do that." She turned and looked out at the afternoon sun touching the tops of the trees, trying to contain her disappointment.

"Good." Troy leaned back in his chair and pulled his sunglasses down over his eyes. She hadn't even noticed them perched on his head. On top of all of his other abilities, he also seemed to be able to shift the way he felt with very little effort. It turned her stomach, realizing that she didn't mean all that much to him. He was just a good man who felt obligated to protect those weaker than he was. Honorable. But not interested in her.

SEVENTEEN

Night fell and brought out the nocturnal creatures that made very different sounds than the ones that roamed in the daylight. The warmth of the afternoon had faded into a light chill. Troy gave Julia and Jake sweatshirts to use if the sleeping bags weren't enough. Jake had gone to sleep, using his as a pillow, likely tired from sheer boredom. Julia was still sitting in the chair. She had gotten up and hobbled around periodically to stretch her legs, but had been quiet for hours. Troy used the night-vision setting on his binoculars to check the area every fifteen to twenty minutes.

He was used to having to be still and alert for extended periods of time. He knew this wouldn't be easy for people who hadn't ever been in a situation like this. Being quiet for so long couldn't have been easy for a ten-year-old boy, but Jake had done well. Julia didn't seem all that interested in talking anymore. She barely even looked at him. It made him wonder what she was thinking. Was she looking forward to putting distance between them? Had he lost her before they'd had a chance to get to know each other outside of this crazy situation?

Maybe that was best. Troy had never intended for Bluerock to be a permanent home. It was always meant to be temporary until he decided what to do next. He turned to Julia, breaking the silence. "Where do you think you'll go when everything gets back to normal?"

She glanced at him then back out into the night. "I don't know. My house is gone. My car went with it. I'm sure I can rent something."

"In Bluerock?" He felt a small surge of hope.

"I don't remember seeing any car rental places in town. I imagine I'll have to find something outside the area." Not what he was hoping to hear.

"Where do you think you'll live?" He waited.

"Maybe my hometown in Connecticut. I haven't seen any of my friends since coming here. I might try forming some kind of reconciliation with my parents. I don't think I'll ever have a great relationship with them, but I'd prefer to at least be on speaking terms."

Troy leaned back in his chair. There was no longer any doubt that she intended to leave. His brief hopes to explore what had sparked between them were fading into the abyss, much like most things that had once mattered to him. It was going to be a long night.

Something shifted in the underbrush, bringing his focus back to the task at hand. He lifted the binoculars and scanned the area. He caught sight of a male form moving toward their location. The man wasn't wearing any night vision, which meant he couldn't see them yet. Troy moved quietly, leaning down to Julia.

He whispered as low as possible. "Someone is down there. Maybe a hundred yards out. I'm going to pick you up and lay you on the sleeping bag." When she nodded, he lifted her and moved her out of sight. He didn't miss the fear in her eyes. It made him want to hold her in his arms and make her feel safe. Unfortunately, he had to focus on what might be coming. And he doubted she was interested in being held by him anyway.

Troy knelt and pulled a leafy blanket over his head. He watched, keeping completely still, as the man approached. The covering came down below his eyebrows and he positioned himself so only his eyes were above the wooden wall of the tree fort. It would appear as though a leafy branch had fallen and gotten caught on the wood. Then he heard someone else moving behind the first man. He watched them come into view and look up at the fort. Troy didn't let a single muscle flinch. The second man looked unsteady on his feet.

The first man turned to his friend. "The ladder's gone."

What were they doing here? Had they been sent to check the area? Would they be reporting back to someone? If they mentioned the ladder being gone, it could bring more competent men up the mountain to double-check in the daylight.

The second man looked up, swaying from side to side. "What'll we do now? I'm too tired to walk back down." His voice was slurry. Was he intoxicated?

"I don't see what choice we have. Unless you want to sleep in the dirt."

Troy tensed. The last thing they needed was for these two to pass out beneath the fort. They wouldn't be able to move or make a sound until the two men woke up and left. And then there would be a greater risk of being seen in the light. Given their demeanor, these men could become aggressive, wanting to get up into the tree fort, as they had planned. It could easily spiral out of control, forcing Troy to hurt them without knowing if they were even involved.

The unsteady man turned in a circle. "Maybe there's another way up. Look for the ladder." He nearly tripped over his own feet.

"We ain't find'n anything in the dark. Let's go. They ain't up here. No one's around. We'd've seen 'em by now." The first man gave the unsteady one a little shove. "C'mon, let's go." They both started moving back down the hill.

Troy stayed completely still for a long time after he heard them move out of range. He used the binoculars to scan the trees and all along the ground. They seemed to be gone, but he was reluctant to make any noise. They had clearly been sent on a scouting mission. Even though they seemed completely incompetent, if they mentioned the missing ladder, it could bring the fight to him. Troy was prepared, but had hoped to avoid it, not wanting Jake to see any more violence. He supposed he would have to take what came and do what he did best.

The sun would be up in a few hours. The two incompetents that had just left could make it down and have someone else head up by then. He looked over at Julia for the first time since he'd put her on the sleeping bag. She looked terrified.

"They're gone. You should get some sleep. I'll keep watch." He didn't want to share his concerns. There was no point in frightening her more than she already was.

"I can watch for a while. You should get some sleep. You'll need your energy if more come." Did she sense what he suspected? He wouldn't have thought it possible, but she had already proven she could think on her feet. She had to have an above average ability to read a situation to have made it through some of the scrapes she'd fought on her own.

"Maybe that would be a good idea. I'll sleep for an hour. But you have to wake me if you hear anything that doesn't fit with what you've been hearing all night. Don't hesitate."

"Believe me, I won't. I have no illusions about what I can and cannot do. I'll get you up if I'm unsure." She pulled herself up and put her hand out. "I should have the binoculars. I'll check every fifteen minutes, like you've been doing." She was definitely paying attention.

He handed them over and leaned back against the tree trunk. He didn't like to be too comfortable in situations where things could escalate suddenly. Being on the periphery of a nap was safer than falling into a deep sleep, which would make jumping into immediate action more challenging.

"Aren't you going to lie down?" Julia moved in front of him.

"No. Can't risk it. I need to be ready." He watched her thick blonde hair fall forward, casting a dark shadow over her face. It was impossible to get a sense of what she was thinking, not being able to see her beautiful eyes.

"I get it. Should I stand or stay low?"

"Low is better. Maybe sit in the chair and keep out of sight. If you see anything, get down and wake me." He closed his eyes, wanting to end the conversation. He knew she'd do what was necessary. He didn't want to risk their voices carrying through the trees. If the men who had been there earlier had heard something, they might come back. Or mention it to someone else.

He heard Julia move slowly back to her chair. He barely heard her sit down. She had been learning from him. She hadn't been this quiet a few days ago. Troy dozed in and out, trying to keep his exhaustion from taking hold. The rhythm of the night made for the perfect white noise to quiet his brain. It all fell away, until something jostled his body.

Troy's eyes popped open, his senses firing immediately. The darkness had begun to dissolve, being replaced by the early light from the rising sun. Julia leaned close, the smell of her shampoo drifting up his nose. She whispered so close to his ear, he could feel the warmth of her breath. He wanted to pull her close and hold her in his arms.

"Someone's coming." Those two words sent a jolt through Troy's body.

Julia handed Troy the binoculars as he scuffled to the side of the fort. Jake sat up and stretched his arms above his head, letting out a long, lazy yawn. Julia quickly put her index finger to her lips as she huddled close to him. Fear immediately filled his eyes. She wrapped her arm around him, hoping to convey calm.

Troy abruptly stood. "We're fine. It's Leo. I forgot to take out the radio yesterday. He's probably here to check on us."

"You told him where we'd be?" Julia was surprised.

"No, but he knows the area at least as well as I do, if not better. It wouldn't be hard for him to come up with some ideas of where I might go." Troy looked through the binoculars again. "He's down a bit. It'll take him another five minutes to get up here."

Jake rose. "I have to pee."

Troy handed him an empty milk carton. "Use this."

Jake stood looking at him. "Can't I go down there?" His finger pointed straight down. "Behind a tree? I won't be able to do that up here. In front of other people." His voice faded with embarrassment.

Troy stood looking at Jake for a moment. "I guess you could do that. Leo is alone. I'll go down with you. You have to stay close to me." When Jake nodded, Troy opened the hatch and threw out the ladder. He started climbing down and stopped with half of his body still sticking up through the square opening. "Julia, are you comfortable staying up here?"

"I'll be fine. Give me the binoculars. I'll let you know if I see someone else coming." She took them from his outstretched hand.

Once the boys were down on the ground, Julia scanned the area. She could see Leo making his way up. She wondered how far down he'd had to park. Not seeing anyone else with him gave her some hope that Troy's faith in his friend might have been warranted. And the man didn't look to be in a hurry. He was walking at a normal pace, not moving like someone trying to sneak in to take down his perceived enemy.

Still, she wanted Jake back up the ladder, with the hatch closed, before Leo got here. She looked and saw Troy waiting by a tree with one of the thickest trunks she had ever seen. Jake was probably on the other side. If she could walk better, she wouldn't be able to stop herself from pacing. The closer Leo got, the faster her heart beat. What was taking so long?

She leaned over the side closest to Troy and

tried to call to him with minimal noise. "He's almost here. What's taking so long?"

Troy shrugged and then turned to the tree. "How's it going in there, buddy?"

"I'm almost done." When Jake answered, without regard for how much noise he was making, Julia looked through the binoculars again. Leo's head jerked up in their direction. If he hadn't been sure before, he knew they were there now.

When Jake finally emerged, Leo was nearly upon them. Jake asked about washing his hands and Troy told him he had disinfectant wipes in the fort. Jake followed Troy back over to the ladder and was about to go up when Leo's voice echoed over the sounds of the birds singing.

"Good morning. I'm really glad to see everyone is alive and well." That jovial voice sent a nearby bird flapping from its perch.

Jake looked up at the chief and his eyes widened as his body froze in place. Julia felt completely helpless, being so high up. She wanted to be down there with Jake. To be there to put him at ease. She saw Jake's foot step back with a slight pivot. Her pulse became an erratic hum through her body. She quickly moved to the hatch and tried to maneuver herself onto the ladder. Not a simple task with the wound still healing in her right thigh.

"Hey, Leo. I know. I know. I didn't turn on the walkie." Troy moved toward his friend, seeming not to notice Jake's sudden panic. "I completely forgot. Some drunks were up here last night scouting the place. I was focused on staying quiet."

Julia made her way down, keeping her eye on Jake. She hadn't seen him that shaken since the first night. She wanted to say something, but wasn't sure she should.

"Yeah, I figured it was something like that. I decided I better come up and have a look myself. Didn't want to see you end up in the hospital again. Or worse." Leo moved closer.

Julia couldn't handle taking such a slow trek and squeezed the ladder together, the way Troy had the day before, and began to slide down. At the bottom, she wasn't able to stop in time to land properly and fell.

Troy saw and ran over to her. "Are you all right? Why did you come down?" He was trying to help her up, but all she could do was attempt to pull away to get to Jake. She knew in her gut that something was wrong.

Leo walked over. "This is why you should come back with me. This is no place for regular civilians, Troy. They have no business trying to make it out here."

"I've got them covered." Troy took a firm stance.

Julia tried to hobble toward Jake. He was edging away. Then his eyes widened even more as Leo turned to fully face him for the first time.

"He shot my dad!" Jake took off running.

Troy turned to see Leo suddenly sprinting after Jake.

Julia's chest tightened, the air suddenly heavy in her lungs. She tried to hobble after them but quickly lost ground.

Troy passed her, running at full speed. But he wasn't fast enough. Leo pushed Jake and he disappeared over the ridge.

EIGHTEEN

Julia's blood-curdling scream tore through the forest, creating a frenzy of activity all around them. Birds were fleeing from the surrounding trees. Squirrels disappeared from sight. Troy was still trying to process what he'd just seen. Had Leo pushed Jake over the edge of the cliff? Had he heard Jake's words correctly? The very idea knocked the wind out of him. The sadness and shock slowed him, hollowing him from his chest down into his gut.

Julia was suddenly at the edge, screaming Jake's name. She was frantic and completely oblivious to Leo's presence. The man Troy had called a friend had murdered an innocent child and was advancing on Julia. Fury threaded through Troy's veins and he jolted back into the soldier he had been. His body moved without thought. He got to Leo, as he was about to shove Julia, and hit the man with such force, he bellowed as his body fell to the ground, five feet away.

Troy stood over Leo, fire burning through him, and pulled out his gun. The chief was a murderer. A criminal. A disgrace to the badge he wore.

Leo put his hands up as he tried to edge backward. "Don't shoot. I'm unarmed. I did this for you, Troy. I've been trying to protect you, but you couldn't just get out of the way."

"Trying to protect me? I was shot, run off the road, attacked. How were you protecting me?" Troy was seething. He could barely get the words out. He could hear Julia behind him, calling Jake's name. Each time, her voice became more desperate, getting closer to the reality that Jake was gone.

Troy stepped closer to Leo, his gun aimed at Leo's chest. "You killed a kid. You killed an *innocent kid*!" He could feel the emotions gripping him from the inside. It wasn't just that he had failed. Jake didn't get to grow up. His mother was alone now. Troy would have to tell her he'd lost her boy to the man who'd taken her husband.

Leo must have sensed Troy's momentary weakness. He stood up. "My guys weren't supposed to touch you. Only the woman and the boy. Never you."

"You think that makes this okay?" Troy raised the gun.

"Hold on. We're still friends. Just let me fix this and we can go back to normal. It'll be like none of this ever happened."

The world began to cloud around them. Troy's vision became like a tunnel, with Leo at the center. "How would you fix it, Leo? Hmm? You think I'm going to let you kill Julia now?" He could feel his tendons tensing, his muscles firing. Every fiber of his being ready.

Troy hadn't heard Julia call Jake's name in more than a minute. He looked over his shoulder, to check on her. She was down on the ground, her body half hanging over the edge. What was she doing?

The distraction was all Leo needed. He tackled Troy, sending the handgun tumbling out of reach. They were well matched in size and Leo had spent years learning to defend himself, making him more of a challenge to Troy than most. They tumbled and punched, each vying for an advantage. Troy felt the stitches in his shoulder tear through his skin.

They grappled until they were both completely winded and standing opposite each other, heaving breaths in and out through their mouths. Troy kept himself positioned to block Julia at all times. It had been a distraction while they'd fought, keeping him from getting the upper hand.

"How could you do this?" Troy gasped out his shame for the man in front of him. "You're supposed to protect people, not send maniacs all over town to kill them."

"Do you have any idea how close this town was to bankruptcy? I brought it back from the brink. I saved this town. You should be thanking me. I brought you here and took you under my wing. Gave you a place to call home while you got your head straight. You have no idea what I've had to do to keep you safe and take care of Bluerock." Leo's tone was a little too indignant. Was it possible that he believed he had done the right thing?

Troy felt a sudden calm filter through him. An understanding of the man before him. As if he had been touched by something greater than himself. His voice came out slow and calm. His breathing returned to normal. "You can tell yourself whatever story you need to. But you know that nothing justifies what you've done. Your citizens live in constant fear. No one will be thanking you for turning this wholesome town into a drug den." Troy stepped closer to him.

"Troy, it's me. Your friend. We've been through too much for it to end this way. Let me do what needs to be done and we can go home." Leo's eyes drifted to Julia.

Troy turned to see her still hanging over the edge of the ridge. He spun back to Leo and realized his old friend had pulled out a gun and was aiming it at Julia. He started running, but a shot rang out before he could get to the man.

The sound of a gun echoed through the valley, sending a ripple a panic through Julia's chest. She turned to see Leo falling to the ground. Troy was standing over him and turning back and forth between her and his friend.

"Are you hit?" he called out to her, confusion clouding his features.

She sat up and felt around. Other than the

wound in her leg and the other injuries she had gotten in Jake's house, she was fine. No bleeding. No additional pain. "No. I'm fine. What about you?" She noticed the blood coming from Leo's stomach as he rolled on his side. "It's him."

Troy knelt down, taking the gun and slipping it into the back of his pants. Then his head jerked up and he scanned the area around them. He pulled the gun back out and took that stance she had seen before, holding the weapon out in front of him.

His voice carried through the trees. "Stop right there. Lower your weapon."

Julia followed his line of sight and saw the policeman who had come to Henry's farm looking for her and Jake, had tried to get to them after her house had exploded, and run Troy off the road. Had he shot Leo? Had he been aiming for Troy? She felt so powerless. She couldn't run. She had no weapon. And she couldn't get to Jake. His legs were visible on a small ledge below, but he wasn't moving. There was no way to know if he was alive or dead. And Troy was facing off with one of the men who had been pursuing them from the beginning. She waited, her breath held in her lungs, unable to move.

The man stood firm, his arms outstretched, his gun pointed at Troy. Neither was going to concede. Julia tried to stand, hoping to find Leo's weapon.

"Don't move." The cop's voice boomed. He turned the gun on her and she froze.

Troy's finger tensed on the trigger. This man could shoot Julia before he went down. Troy couldn't turn to see where Julia was. He couldn't risk taking his eyes off the cop who had nearly killed him. Had Leo lied about the guy's condition? The man in front of him didn't look any worse for the wear.

"I'm not here to hurt you. I've been trying to get to you before they did. I'm DEA. I've been here undercover for six months." He took a few steps forward. Troy kept his sights on the center of the man's chest.

"You expect me to believe that? You tried to kill me."

"No, I tried to get you to pull over so we could talk, and our tires caught together. Then we spun off the road. There was nothing I could do to prevent it. I'm the one that called for an ambulance. I could have killed you then. You were unconscious." Troy replayed the accident in his head. From this new perspective, he could see the possibility of it being true.

"Can you prove it?" Troy kept alert.

"Well, I can't exactly carry around my real ID. I'm Adam Hayes. I was the person helping the kid's father." He began to lower his weapon. "I'm going to put this away now. Will you do the same?"

That was the name Julia had mentioned after meeting Jake's mother. Either he was telling the truth or he had gotten the information from Jake's father before he'd been killed. Troy waited until the gun was in its holster, then he lowered his own, but kept it in his hand. He noticed Leo trying to slink away and walked over to stop him.

"Julia, tell me if he moves." He nodded at the man claiming to be Adam Hayes. He then knelt down and twisted Leo's hand behind his back, forcing him onto his wounded belly. Leo grunted in pain as Troy secured his hands.

Leo jerked his head up, trying to turn over. "You're dead, *Adam*. Or whatever your name is. When the guys find out who you really are, they'll come for you." A losing man's last attempt to hold on to his power.

Adam actually laughed as he walked forward. He didn't even acknowledged Leo. "Where's the kid? I told his father his family would be safe. Everything went sideways when the kid confided in one of his guys." He tipped his head at Leo. "I've been trying to make it right ever since. That's why I've been pursuing you. I figured we'd do better as a team. I've heard a lot of stories about you. I have to admit, you're even better than they said." He held out his hand.

Troy shook it, letting this new information settle in his mind. It would have been helpful to have someone else on their side. He had thought so from the beginning, but hadn't wanted to risk trusting the wrong person. Clearly, he had failed at that, too. He had trusted Leo.

"How did you know where to find us?" Troy tensed again, waiting for an answer.

"I followed him." He gestured at Leo. "I started keeping tabs on him after the accident. I knew he'd eventually come himself. His guys were screwing it up and it was only a matter of time before he decided to put an end to things."

Leo's hateful glare added some validity to what the man was saying, but Leo had proven how deceitful he could be. Then Julia's scream cut through his thoughts and echoed across the valley below. Something was wrong. The screech in her voice was desperate.

Troy turned to go then hesitated. He stared at the man calling himself a DEA agent. He didn't want to risk being shot in the back. But he had to get to Julia. Then Adam pulled out his gun and raised the barrel in his direction. Troy froze.

NINETEEN

Adam let his gun turn over and rest in his palm, extending his arm, handing it over to Troy. "Will you let me help you?" He gestured toward Julia. "Let's go."

Troy took the gun and stuck it in the back of his pants as they ran together. Troy dropped to the ground next to Julia. "What's wrong?"

"He moved! He's alive! We have to get him!" Julia pointed down to a small rock ledge, where Jake's legs were visible.

Troy could see Jake's knees bending. It wasn't much, but it was something. He looked around for what he could use to lower himself down.

Adam peered over the edge. "I could help you down and pull you back up." When Troy's expression was skeptical, Adam rolled his eyes. "Lower *me*, then. If I do anything to hurt the kid, you can shoot me." He stared at Troy, clearly becoming frustrated with Troy's lack of trust.

Troy eyed him. "Fine. You go down. Don't think I won't do it."

He lowered the other man to the ledge. Julia was practically falling over the side, frantic with worry.

"I need you to move back. I can't pull them up if I'm stopping you from falling." He didn't mean to be harsh, but Adam wasn't light and Troy's energy was waning. She moved back and waited.

Adam dropped to his knees and looked Jake over. Troy couldn't get a full view, making him uneasy. "Is he awake?" he called down.

"Not fully, but he's coming around. I'm going to check him over before I move him." Adam slowly felt around for injuries and then looked up. "He's waking up."

Troy exhaled, feeling hopeful. He turned his eyes toward the sky. *Let him be all right.*

Adam's voice brought his attention back to the ledge.

"I'm going to lift him up to you." Adam pulled Jake over his shoulder and stood. Then he lifted Jake above his head, to where Troy could reach him.

Jake looked a little dazed, but he was reaching for Troy. He grabbed the boy's forearms and pulled him up. Julia was by his side a moment later. As Troy laid him on the ground, Jake's eyes rolled closed and his head fell to the side.

"No, no, no. Wake up, Jake. Please, open your eyes." Julia was distraught. Tears began streaming down her cheeks. "Jake!" She fell over him, crying.

She became lost in grief. Every hope she had of getting Jake back to his mother was lost. Troy had done everything possible and it still hadn't been enough. She could hear Troy assisting the DEA agent, but didn't bother looking.

"You're crushing me." Jake's voice was barely more than a whisper.

Julia jolted upright and saw that his eyes were open. Adam Hayes pulled out a penlight and checked Jake's eyes. Troy watched, with caution, appearing to be as upset as she was.

"He looks good. We can get him checked

out in town. I'm assuming you have a way down?" Adam looked at Troy.

"I have a Ranger tucked in the bushes. I'll take them. You get Leo." Troy helped Julia up and then bent down to lift Jake into his arms. Adam dragged Leo to his unsteady feet and forced him forward.

Julia wondered how they would all fit. There was one bench seat with barely enough room for three people. She followed Troy into the bushes and watched him place Jake into the middle of the seat and then put his seat belt on.

He looked up at her. "I'll pull it out, but you're driving. I need to watch our surroundings." When she nodded, he got in and backed the Ranger out for her.

She got into the driver's seat and waited while Troy pulled the cap off the bed in the back. She turned and watched Adam and Troy pull Leo onto the bed. She looked forward and clasped her hands together under her chin. *Thank you, Lord, for bringing help and keeping Jake alive. Please let this be the end of this nightmare.*

Adam's voice came from behind her. "I'll sit back here with him. You ride with them."

Julia looked and saw him tilt his head at the interior of the Ranger.

Troy nodded. "Fine. If he tries anything, shoot him."

"After all I've done for you, this is how you repay me? It's not too late, Troy. You can do the right thing." Leo's voice was strained but still held a surprising amount of hubris.

Troy moved in close, grabbing his old friend by the collar of his shirt. "You're done. You can stop pretending we're friends." He stepped back and looked at Adam. "Ready?"

When Adam bobbed his head, Troy got in next to Jake. Julia drove slow, trying to avoid too much jostling. There was no way to know how hard Jake had hit his head or what injuries might be lurking inside his body. She had heard her father talk about patients who'd looked fine on the outside, but he had found major problems once he'd run tests and opened them up. Her father sometimes assisted in the emergency room. He'd said it was his way to help some of the people who would never have been able to afford him otherwise. It had always been one of the few things she'd admired about him.

When they reached the halfway point,

Julia saw Leo's police cruiser parked off to the side. He had walked a long way to get to them. And so had Adam. She heard a loud whistle and realized it had come from the back of the Ranger. Troy twisted his head, glaring through the back window. Then he turned to her.

"Something's up. Keep driving." She saw him scanning the area around them.

Shots rang out, echoing from every direction. Julia sank down as low as she could, then reached over and unlatched Jake's seatbelt. She didn't even have to tell him. He slid down to the floor in front of Troy, curling into a ball. She tried to go faster. The Ranger jerked and bumped, making it difficult to steer. She had to slow down. They would end up flipping over if she continued this way.

Risking a glance to her left, she saw a man taking aim at *her*. Tension tightened her body. A shot rang out. She braced for impact, knowing exactly how much it would hurt. When it didn't come, she looked over and saw that the man was down. She turned to Troy. He pointed to Adam. The man they'd thought had been hunting them had saved her life. Any doubts she had about him evaporated.

Leo was grumbling obscenities behind her. Troy turned forward. "I think we're clear." He helped Jake back into the middle of the bench seat and refastened his seatbelt.

Julia kept driving, wondering what would happen when they got to the bottom of the mountain. They still had no idea how many were involved in this operation. While they finally had some help, two men weren't enough against a small criminal army.

As she reached the main road, her foot slammed on the brake. Five black SUVs whizzed by, one after the other. Had someone called in reinforcements? Was this bigger than the people in Bluerock? Was a cartel involved? They could be rolling in to take control, fully prepared with men and weapons.

Julia jolted when she felt a hand on her shoulder. She turned and saw Troy smiling at her. What did that mean?

"Everything will be fine. Keep going. I promise you're safe now." His light touch put her at ease. She rolled out onto the pavement and followed the black vehicles to the Bluerock police station. It was a small brick building set back from Main Street. The SUVs all stopped out front. She pulled in behind the last one, parking in front of a small pizzeria.

Troy got out and started walking up the sidewalk.

A man exited the last SUV and Troy advanced. His eyes were as intense as Troy's always were. They had a similar build and comportment. Troy held out his hand. The man took it and then pulled Troy into an embrace. His features softened, a smile forming on his lips. They were talking, but with all of the activity around them, it was impossible to hear. She could feel the Ranger shift then saw Adam dragging Leo toward Troy. The other man reached into the back seat of the SUV and pulled out a dark windbreaker. When he put it on and turned, she saw the letters FBI emblazoned on the back. Had this been Troy's plan?

Troy motioned to Julia and the two men walked up to her. "Julia, I'd like you to meet Todd Spencer. He's an old friend. I sent him the video and he brought the help we needed."

"It's very nice to meet you. And to see some law enforcement we can trust." Julia, relieved, was more interested in having Jake checked out. She looked down at him, sleeping with his head resting on her shoulder. "We need to get him to the ER."

"We already have an ambulance on the way. It's very nice to meet you, Julia. Troy has told me some pretty impressive things about you." Todd had a gentler demeanor than Troy, but a very similar strong presence. She felt heat burn up her neck and cheeks at hearing that Troy had been talking about her in a fond way. It made her feel a little silly.

Things moved quickly after that. An ambulance came for Jake and Julia insisted on going with him. She had no idea what was happening with the local police or how the FBI fit in to all of this. Would the DEA take over? It was a drug case. She didn't know enough about either agency to fully speculate how things would be handled. All she knew was that Troy stayed with them. He hadn't come with her and Jake. That seemed like a clear message to her. He had done his job. She and Jake were safe. There was an FBI agent watching over them now. Troy wasn't interested in being in her company now that he didn't need to protect her. The thought of it made her a little sad.

At least she knew Jake would be all right.

After running a battery of tests, the doctors concluded he had no serious injuries. Julia looked over his chart, still knowing how to read the results. She took Jake in the wheelchair to see his mother as soon as the doctor gave her consent. She stepped out into the hall to give them some time alone.

The FBI agent stayed close, but didn't crowd her. She leaned against the wall and closed her eyes. She thanked God for their safety. For giving them everything they'd needed throughout this ordeal. For allowing them to survive to see it through to the end. So much had happened, it was impossible to specify each situation, but she tried.

Now that she knew there was no reason to stay in Bluerock, Julia began considering her options. Surviving so much had given her a different appreciation for her life. She had no intention of hiding anymore. She was going to get back out into the world and find her place. It didn't seem so scary anymore. Not in comparison to all that she had survived in Bluerock. But this town felt more like home than anywhere else. She wanted to help where she was able. And she could see a future here. With or without Troy in her life.

* * *

Troy watched men he had spent time with being arrested. He had been so lost in his own head, he hadn't noticed what had been happening right under his nose. And now this town was imploding. Most of the police force, along with several local business owners, had already been arrested. If someone didn't step up, Bluerock would become one of those ghost towns people visited to see where it had all happened, that would eventually crumble and be forgotten. There were so many good people still living there. What would happen to them?

He had barely had the chance to introduce Julia to Todd before she'd left with Jake. He'd wanted to explain that he had sent the video Jake's father had made to his friend and set something in motion to bring about a resolution. It had happened even faster than he'd expected. He stood in the police station, a flurry of activity swirling around him as the FBI and DEA worked to piece together what had been going on and who had been involved.

The local police, including Troy's good friend Leo, and some local business owners, had gotten involved in producing drugs in an abandoned warehouse and had set up a network of people to distribute them outside the area. It had worked well. No one would have ever thought to look to Bluerock as the source. Everything was sold outside the county. There would be a series of arrests over the next several weeks in Pennsylvania, New Jersey and New York. All of this being brought to light because Jake's father had been brave enough to do something about it. He had reached out to a DEA agent and taken a video to prove his allegations. His loss was a tragedy. The man was a hero, as far as Troy was concerned.

The whole thing felt like a bad dream that was finally ending. All he could think of was going to see Julia and Jake. He had been asked to stay back and assist, given his knowledge of the town and his direct involvement, but he had shared all that he'd known. He needed to see them. There wasn't much more he could do at the station. He had to tell Julia what was going on. More importantly, she needed to know how he felt about her. She had become his world and he had to know if she felt the same.

The ride to the hospital was short and he

moved through the building with purpose. When he found Jake's room empty, a sliver of panic began to turn his stomach before he remembered that Jake's mother was on another floor. He didn't wait for the elevator. Instead, he took the stairs, two at a time. When he reached Jake's mother's floor and stepped into the hallway, he saw Julia leaning against the wall with her eyes closed. She was the most beautiful woman he had ever seen. And her heart was so pure. He just stood for a moment, watching her.

When Julia opened her eyes and stepped away from the wall, she turned his way. Troy's stomach tightened with anticipation. Her smile made everything else fall away. His feet took him forward without thought. Then she was in his arms. He pulled her close and his eyes drifted upward. *Thank you, Lord, for bringing us through this. I know I've been distant for a while, but I always believed in You. I just needed a little time to find my way.*

Troy stepped back but kept his hands on Julia's arms. "How's Jake? Are *you* okay? How's your leg?"

Julia smiled up at him. "Jake is fine. He's in with his mother. I'm fine, too. How about you? I know it had to be hard for you to turn Leo in."

He shook his head. "No. He isn't the man I knew. What he tried to do to you and Jake…" Troy took a steadying breath, pushing the thought away. "He belongs in jail." He proceeded to tell Julia all that he had learned and what would be happening next, including multiple arrests in three different states. Julia seemed stunned by the magnitude of the operation.

She was quiet for a moment. "It's hard to imagine any of that happening in a place like this. But when I think back to things I saw, what you're telling me fits. I was just too wrapped up in what I was doing to realize something was off. But it's over now. By the grace of God, we managed to keep Jake safe. I'm just so grateful to Him for bringing you to us that morning. He kept showing us He was there, even when we had our doubts. I don't know how I could ever repay you for everything you've done."

Troy took her hands in his. "You never have to thank me. I wanted to help you and Jake. That kid has become like family to me. And you…" He swallowed the emotion behind the words. "You've become so much more. I've fallen in love with you. I can't imagine my life without you. I know we haven't known each other long, but I've never felt this way for anyone before. I'm hoping you don't plan on leaving town. I've been asked to step in to run the police department until everything is sorted. But if you'd rather not stay here, I'd be willing to go anywhere to be with you."

Julia's lips parted but she didn't say anything. Maybe she didn't feel the same way? Maybe she didn't want to stay in Bluerock? Then the corners of her mouth lifted and her eyes moistened with unshed tears.

"I think I'd like to stay here with you. This town welcomed me in a way my own family never has. And I've fallen in love with you, too." She smiled up at him as a lone tear rolled down her cheek.

Troy slid his hands along the sides of her face, wiping the tear away with the pad of his thumb, and leaned down, pressing his lips to hers. He felt the love they now shared running between them. He could never have imagined he could be this happy after so much turmoil. But he was happy. And he had found the love of his life.

EPILOGUE

It had been nearly a full month since the FBI and DEA had rolled into Bluerock and brought order back to a town torn apart by the people who had sworn to protect it. Troy played a role in creating a new police force, recruiting good men and women from various surrounding counties. The citizens were scared at first; they had no idea whether their little town would survive. Some packed up and moved away, tired of living in fear. Now that the corrupt police weren't watching, they had the freedom to leave. Most wanted to see their town restored and stayed.

Becoming a part of this community had filled Troy with purpose. Being with Julia had given him something he hadn't experienced since he was a teenager. Her love filled him and brought light back into his life. She helped him continue to rebuild his relationship with God, which enabled him to stop searching for the darkness in everyone he met.

Jake's mother had been moved to the rehabilitation unit of the hospital. She was nearly ready to go home. Some people from the church had cleaned and repaired her house. A collection had been taken to pay off the mortgage. Her husband had lost his life trying to put a stop to the drug trade that had nearly destroyed the town. Troy took some comfort in knowing Jake and his mother would be all right. Julia had promised his mother that she would look after Jake until the woman was able to come home and care for her son.

Troy had offered for them to stay at his lake house when Jake was released from the hospital. He had spent every day with them.

Today was no different. He knocked on the door before walking in. There were smells inside that made his mouth water. Julia looked up and smiled from the kitchen.

"You're just in time. I made a late lunch. And there's an apple crisp in the oven." She moved around his kitchen like it was her own. Troy didn't want anyone else in that kitchen.

To him, it was Julia's. She had made him so many delicious meals and desserts, continually expressing her gratitude for all that he had done. If he wasn't careful, he was going to lose his fit physique.

After they ate and Jake had settled in front of the TV to work on a Welcome Home banner for his mother, Troy asked Julia to take a walk down to the lake. As they strolled along, Julia told him all about her plans to partner with a dessert company that wanted to sell her pastries. She planned to turn the old warehouse into something that would benefit the town. It would become her base of operations and provide jobs. She was always thinking of ways to help everyone.

When they reached the edge of the dock, Troy turned to her and held her face in his palms, looking directly into her mossy-green eyes. "I love you, Julia. I'd like you to stay here. You make this house feel like a real home. And once we're married, I want it to be our home."

"Married?" Her mouth fell open in surprise.

Troy got down on one knee in front of her and took her left hand in his. "I know this may feel a little sudden, but I've never felt this way about anyone or anything in my life. I know I want you to be my wife, when you're ready. I want to create a family with you. Will you share your life with me?" He watched her wide eyes stare down at him. Had he made a mistake? Was he pushing for too much too soon?

Then she lowered her forehead to his. "I never thought I could love anyone the way I love you. I don't think it's sudden at all. Yes, of course, I'll marry you." Her words lit him up from the inside. He stood and pulled her into his arms, kissing her again. Savoring the way she made him feel. He was going to spend every day building a life with her. Troy had never imagined he could experience this much love or happiness. Everything they had endured had brought them together. And he had no intention of ever letting go.

* * * * *

*Find strength and determination in stories
of faith and love in the face of danger.*

*Look for six new releases every month,
available wherever Love Inspired Suspense
books and ebooks are sold.*

*Find more great reads at
www.LoveInspired.com*

Dear Reader,

Thank you for sharing Julia and Troy's journey. Their travels were difficult and they both had traumas we don't all experience. Many children grow up with uncertainty, even when things don't appear that way from the outside. When I was a teacher, it wasn't always easy to provide what children from homes like these really needed. There are so many soldiers who come home looking the same but feeling broken inside. These courageous men and women have to work hard to find their way back to a healthy balance. My hope is that people will look to God for what they need when the world proves lacking, as it does for so many of us. Without Him, it's too easy to get lost.

Warm regards,
Addie Ellis

Get 3 FREE REWARDS!

We'll send you 2 FREE Books plus a FREE Mystery Gift.

FREE Value Over **$20**

Both the **Love Inspired®** and **Love Inspired® Suspense** series feature compelling novels filled with inspirational romance, faith, forgiveness and hope.

YES! Please send me 2 FREE novels from the Love Inspired or Love Inspired Suspense series and my FREE gift (gift is worth about $10 retail). After receiving them, if I don't wish to receive any more books, I can return the shipping statement marked "cancel." If I don't cancel, I will receive 6 brand-new Love Inspired Larger-Print books or Love Inspired Suspense Larger-Print books every month and be billed just $6.49 each in the U.S. or $6.74 each in Canada. That is a savings of at least 16% off the cover price. It's quite a bargain! Shipping and handling is just 50¢ per book in the U.S. and $1.25 per book in Canada.* I understand that accepting the 2 free books and gift places me under no obligation to buy anything. I can always return a shipment and cancel at any time by calling the number below. The free books and gift are mine to keep no matter what I decide.

Choose one:
☐ **Love Inspired Larger-Print** (122/322 BPA GRPA)
☐ **Love Inspired Suspense Larger-Print** (107/307 BPA GRPA)
☐ **Or Try Both!** (122/322 & 107/307 BPA GRRP)

Name (please print)

Address   Apt. #

City   State/Province   Zip/Postal Code

Email: Please check this box ☐ if you would like to receive newsletters and promotional emails from Harlequin Enterprises ULC and its affiliates. You can unsubscribe anytime.

Mail to the Harlequin Reader Service:
IN U.S.A.: P.O. Box 1341, Buffalo, NY 14240-8531
IN CANADA: P.O. Box 603, Fort Erie, Ontario L2A 5X3

Want to try 2 free books from another series? Call 1-800-873-8635 or visit www.ReaderService.com.

---

*Terms and prices subject to change without notice. Prices do not include sales taxes, which will be charged (if applicable) based on your state or country of residence. Canadian residents will be charged applicable taxes. Offer not valid in Quebec. This offer is limited to one order per household. Books received may not be as shown. Not valid for current subscribers to the Love Inspired or Love Inspired Suspense series. All orders subject to approval. Credit or debit balances in a customer's account(s) may be offset by any other outstanding balance owed by or to the customer. Please allow 4 to 6 weeks for delivery. Offer available while quantities last.

Your Privacy—Your information is being collected by Harlequin Enterprises ULC, operating as Harlequin Reader Service. For a complete summary of the information we collect, how we use this information and to whom it is disclosed, please visit our privacy notice located at corporate.harlequin.com/privacy-notice. From time to time we may also exchange your personal information with reputable third parties. If you wish to opt out of this sharing of your personal information, please visit readerservice.com/consumerschoice or call 1-800-873-8635. **Notice to California Residents**—Under California law, you have specific rights to control and access your data. For more information on these rights and how to exercise them, visit corporate.harlequin.com/california-privacy.

LIRLIS23

Get 3 FREE REWARDS!

We'll send you 2 FREE Books <u>plus</u> a FREE Mystery Gift.

FREE Value Over **$20**

Both the **Harlequin® Special Edition** and **Harlequin® Heartwarming™** series feature compelling novels filled with stories of love and strength where the bonds of friendship, family and community unite.

YES! Please send me 2 FREE novels from the Harlequin Special Edition or Harlequin Heartwarming series and my FREE Gift (gift is worth about $10 retail). After receiving them, if I don't wish to receive any more books, I can return the shipping statement marked "cancel." If I don't cancel, I will receive 6 brand-new Harlequin Special Edition books every month and be billed just $5.49 each in the U.S. or $6.24 each in Canada, a savings of at least 12% off the cover price, or 4 brand-new Harlequin Heartwarming Larger-Print books every month and be billed just $6.24 each in the U.S. or $6.74 each in Canada, a savings of at least 19% off the cover price. It's quite a bargain! Shipping and handling is just 50¢ per book in the U.S. and $1.25 per book in Canada.* I understand that accepting the 2 free books and gift places me under no obligation to buy anything. I can always return a shipment and cancel at any time by calling the number below. The free books and gift are mine to keep no matter what I decide.

Choose one: ☐ **Harlequin Special Edition** (235/335 BPA GRMK)   ☐ **Harlequin Heartwarming Larger-Print** (161/361 BPA GRMK)   ☐ **Or Try Both!** (235/335 & 161/361 BPA GRPZ)

Name (please print)

Address   Apt. #

City   State/Province   Zip/Postal Code

Email: Please check this box ☐ if you would like to receive newsletters and promotional emails from Harlequin Enterprises ULC and its affiliates. You can unsubscribe anytime.

> Mail to the **Harlequin Reader Service:**
> **IN U.S.A.:** P.O. Box 1341, Buffalo, NY 14240-8531
> **IN CANADA:** P.O. Box 603, Fort Erie, Ontario L2A 5X3
>
> **Want to try 2 free books from another series!** Call 1-800-873-8635 or visit www.ReaderService.com.

*Terms and prices subject to change without notice. Prices do not include sales taxes, which will be charged (if applicable) based on your state or country of residence. Canadian residents will be charged applicable taxes. Offer not valid in Quebec. This offer is limited to one order per household. Books received may not be as shown. Not valid for current subscribers to the Harlequin Special Edition or Harlequin Heartwarming series. All orders subject to approval. Credit or debit balances in a customer's account(s) may be offset by any other outstanding balance owed by or to the customer. Please allow 4 to 6 weeks for delivery. Offer available while quantities last.

Your Privacy—Your information is being collected by Harlequin Enterprises ULC, operating as Harlequin Reader Service. For a complete summary of the information we collect, how we use this information and to whom it is disclosed, please visit our privacy notice located at corporate.harlequin.com/privacy-notice. From time to time we may also exchange your personal information with reputable third parties. If you wish to opt out of this sharing of your personal information, please visit readerservice.com/consumerschoice or call 1-800-873-8635. Notice to California Residents—Under California law, you have specific rights to control and access your data. For more information on these rights and how to exercise them, visit corporate.harlequin.com/california-privacy.

HSEHW23

Get 3 FREE REWARDS!

We'll send you 2 FREE Books plus a FREE Mystery Gift.

FREE
Value Over
$20

Both the **Mystery Library** and **Essential Suspense** series feature compelling novels filled with gripping mysteries, edge-of-your-seat thrillers and heart-stopping romantic suspense stories.

YES! Please send me 2 FREE novels from the Mystery Library or Essential Suspense Collection and my FREE Gift (gift is worth about $10 retail). After receiving them, if I don't wish to receive any more books, I can return the shipping statement marked "cancel." If I don't cancel, I will receive 4 brand-new Mystery Library books every month and be billed just $6.74 each in the U.S. or $7.24 each in Canada, a savings of at least 25% off the cover price, or 4 brand-new Essential Suspense books every month and be billed just $7.49 each in the U.S. or $7.74 each in Canada, a savings of at least 17% off the cover price. It's quite a bargain! Shipping and handling is just 50¢ per book in the U.S. and $1.25 per book in Canada.* I understand that accepting the 2 free books and gift places me under no obligation to buy anything. I can always return a shipment and cancel at any time by calling the number below. The free books and gift are mine to keep no matter what I decide.

Choose one: ☐ **Mystery Library** (414/424 BPA GRPM) ☐ **Essential Suspense** (191/391 BPA GRPM) ☐ **Or Try Both!** (414/424 & 191/391 BPA GRRZ)

Name (please print)

Address   Apt. #

City   State/Province   Zip/Postal Code

Email: Please check this box ☐ if you would like to receive newsletters and promotional emails from Harlequin Enterprises ULC and its affiliates. You can unsubscribe anytime.

> Mail to the **Harlequin Reader Service:**
> **IN U.S.A.:** P.O. Box 1341, Buffalo, NY 14240-8531
> **IN CANADA:** P.O. Box 603, Fort Erie, Ontario L2A 5X3

Want to try 2 free books from another series? Call 1-800-873-8635 or visit www.ReaderService.com.

---

*Terms and prices subject to change without notice. Prices do not include sales taxes, which will be charged (if applicable) based on your state or country of residence. Canadian residents will be charged applicable taxes. Offer not valid in Quebec. This offer is limited to one order per household. Books received may not be as shown. Not valid for current subscribers to the Mystery Library or Essential Suspense Collection. All orders subject to approval. Credit or debit balances in a customer's account(s) may be offset by any other outstanding balance owed by or to the customer. Please allow 4 to 6 weeks for delivery. Offer available while quantities last.

Your Privacy—Your information is being collected by Harlequin Enterprises ULC, operating as Harlequin Reader Service. For a complete summary of the information we collect, how we use this information and to whom it is disclosed, please visit our privacy notice located at corporate.harlequin.com/privacy-notice. From time to time we may also exchange your personal information with reputable third parties. If you wish to opt out of this sharing of your personal information, please visit readerservice.com/consumerchoice or call 1-800-873-8635. **Notice to California Residents**—Under California law, you have specific rights to control and access your data. For more information on these rights and how to exercise them, visit corporate.harlequin.com/california-privacy.

MYSSTS23

COMING NEXT MONTH FROM
Love Inspired Suspense

ALASKAN WILDERNESS RESCUE
K-9 Search and Rescue • by Sarah Varland

A search for a missing hiker goes disastrously wrong when K-9 search and rescuer Elsie Montgomery and pilot Wyatt Chandler find themselves stranded on a remote Alaskan island. Only they're not alone. But is this a rescue mission...or a deadly trap?

DANGEROUS TEXAS HIDEOUT
Cowboy Protectors • by Virginia Vaughan

When her daughter is the only witness able to identify a group of bank robbers, Penny Jackson knows their lives are in danger. Escaping to a small Texas town was supposed to be safe, but now they must rely on police chief Caleb Harmon to protect them from a killer bent on silencing them...

DEADLY MOUNTAIN ESCAPE
by Mary Alford

Attempting to find a kidnapped woman and expose a human trafficking ring nearly costs Deputy Charlotte Walker her life. But rancher Jonas Knowles saves her, and they work together to locate the others who have been abducted. Can they survive the onslaught of armed criminals *and* the perilous wilderness?

TARGETED FOR ELIMINATION
by Jill Elizabeth Nelson

A morning jog becomes an exercise in terror when Detective Jen Blackwell is ambushed—until her ex-boyfriend Tyler Cade rescues her. Only someone is targeting them both, forcing Jen to team up with the park ranger to uncover the mystery behind the attacks...before it costs them their lives.

WYOMING ABDUCTION THREAT
by Elisabeth Rees

There's only one thing stopping Sheriff Brent Fox from adopting his foster children: his adoption caseworker. But Carly Engelman has very good reasons for caution—all of which disappear when the children's ruthless biological father returns to abduct his kids...with revenge and murder on his mind.

SILENCING THE WITNESS
by Laura Conaway

Avery Sanford thought she was safe in witness protection...until her photo was leaked in the local paper. Now vengeful cartel members are on her tail and only former army commander Seth Brown can help her. But with assailants anticipating their every move, can Avery trust Seth to keep her alive long enough to testify?

LOOK FOR THESE AND OTHER LOVE INSPIRED BOOKS WHEREVER BOOKS ARE SOLD, INCLUDING MOST BOOKSTORES, SUPERMARKETS, DISCOUNT STORES AND DRUGSTORES.

LISCNM1223